The Boy Who Was Girl

The Boy Who Was Girl

David Gerrold

Star Traveler Press

ISBN-13: 979-8-9925058-5-6 (paperback)

ISBN-13: 979-8-9925058-6-3 (eBook)

The Boy Who Was Girl copyright © 2025 by David Gerrold

Editor and Publisher: Justin T. O'Conor Sloane
Cover art: *Bolo Observation Platform* © 2025 by Marianne Plumridge
Book design by Katerina Bruno

Published by Star Traveler Press
an imprint of Starship Sloane Publishing Company, Inc.
Austin-Round Rock Metro, Texas, USA
starshipsloane.com

Printed in the United States of America & internationally

CONTENTS

FOREWORD

D avid Gerrold understands shapeshifters . . . and he should.

Throughout his writing career, he has frequently morphed, shifting from one extraordinary creative vision to another. In the mid-1960s, he wrote the screenplay for one of the most well-received episodes of *Star Trek* ever, "The Trouble with Tribbles." In the 70s, he wrote for the Saturday morning live-action fantasy TV series *Land of the Lost*, even creating the lizard-like Sleestak race at the heart of the show's mythology. On the prose fiction side, he wrote the sci-fi novels *The Martian Child, The Man Who Folded Himself,* and *When HARLIE Was One*, plus the *Star Wolf* and *War Against the Chtorr* series.

When it comes to his work, Gerrold never stops shifting for long, much like Slither, the protagonist of his novella, *The Boy Who Was Girl.* Maybe that's why he does such a great job bringing Slither to life in a believable and sympathetic way . . . no mean feat, considering Slither can be a stone-cold killer and even a cannibal when they need to be.

Gerrold portrays Slither and their transformations in ways that feel realistic, with great attention to detail. Early on, they talk about the popular image of these literal change agents: "Most folks think shifters are like amoebas—that we're boneless blobs of human gelatin, flowing into this shape or that like so much warm pudding poured into a mold." The popular perception, it turns out, is nothing like the reality, and Gerrold, through Slither, proceeds to set the record straight.

When Slither talks about eating to build up body mass, giving them something to work with when reshaping their form, it seems like the kind of approach a shapeshifter would naturally employ to make a change possible without completely disregarding all laws of physics. It makes sense, after all, that extra mass couldn't just materialize out of thin air, that a shifter would have to obtain it from somewhere to take on a form that was bigger or bulkier than their current physique.

Assuming such limitations exist, it also seems realistic that a shapeshifter would not always miraculously overcome every threat to their safety and freedom. Gerrold explores that very notion and uses it to humanize Slither, putting them through one challenge after another on the road to whatever destiny awaits them. With a little bad luck in the mix, they can be captured, restrained, weakened, and brutalized, going through hell in spite of their superhuman augmentations . . . and experiencing relatable feelings in the process.

Imagining the mindset of such a being in a way that feels authentic could be a major challenge for a lesser writer, but Gerrold handles it with the skill of a longtime creator with extraordinary chops and chameleonic tendencies of his own. As he has done so often in other works, he grounds his extraordinary lead character in thoughts and emotions much like our own, reactions that rope us into rooting for Slither on their dangerous journey no matter how many times they get their hands dirty along the way.

Even as we get comfortable with this complex character and engrossed in their story, Gerrold slips a message in under the radar about identity and tolerance.

To anyone who's a regular reader (or viewer) of Gerrold's work (and his online posts), this message should come as no surprise. Exploring the differences between us—and finding common ground—is a theme he often returns to.

Slither is the embodiment of the old saying, "You can't judge a book by its cover." No one but Slither (and the reader privy to their thoughts) can ever be 100% certain of what's happening under their skin. Absent the use of sophisticated scanning techniques, Slither's true nature can be surprising—and dangerous, often fatal—indeed.

In this way, *The Boy Who Was Girl* harkens back to Gerrold's first *Star Trek* script. The title creatures in "The Trouble with Tribbles" seem like harmless, adorable furballs . . . but their appearance is *very* deceiving. Once the tribbles gorge on grain, they go into a breeding hyperdrive that puts the most fertile of rabbits to shame.

Like tribbles, Slither presents a misleading outward appearance that conceals dangerous tendencies. We're still drawn to sympathize with them, though, because of the good intentions that coexist with the darkness and methodical cruelty of which they're capable in pursuit of their objectives.

Maybe Slither's fluid notions of identity also play a role. As suggested by the title of Gerrold's novella, Slither is capable of shifting between genders, switching from male to female and back (with some difficulty) according to the requirements of their mission. They, and others like them, see gender as just another malleable characteristic that can be altered as needed, much like hair color, facial structure, musculature, and height.

In Slither's sponsor organization, gender changes are taken lightly and not regarded as anything unusual or undesirable. As Slither says of their boss—first identified as "The Old Man" and later as "Mom"—"BTW, she's not an old man—at least, not this year."

Slither has their own preference and talks about it matter-of-factly. "I like being female," they say, "even though it isn't my native gender."

What happens, in the course of their adventures, when Gerrold drops such a gender-fluid character into a rigidly all-male monoculture on the distant world of Sparta? On the surface, a battle of the multifarious versus the uniform; underneath, perhaps, a metaphor for our times.

Current political tides reflect a push for uniformity and adherence to what some consider norms of personal identity. There are those, like the monocultural males of Sparta, who advocate limiting available gender roles and restricting inclusivity. It's the same conflict that's been replayed, in one way or another, throughout human history.

Will limitations on personal choice dominate the future, choking off social constructs that aim to embrace and even cultivate a diversified culture with a multitude of choices and viewpoints?

Gerrold's preference seems clear in Slither's tale . . . and shares more than a passing resemblance with a key theme of the TV series that was home to some of his most inspired writing.

At the heart of the original *Star Trek* was a philosophy—espoused by Mr. Spock and the Vulcan race—known as IDIC, or "Infinite Diversity in Infinite Combinations." In the episode "Is There in Truth No Beauty?" it was best expressed by Miranda Jones (Diana Muldaur): "The glory of creation is in its infinite diversity," and Mr. Spock (Leonard Nimoy): "And the ways our differences combine to create meaning and beauty."[1]

It's not exactly a new concept, yet it still has the power to change entire worlds in *The Boy Who Was Girl*. When Slither, a being of a thousand faces, fights for their life and the fate of endangered worlds, the power of change makes a formidable force for good against an inflexible enemy.

It's a hopeful, enlightened twist in a tale filled with ugliness, suffering, and abuse. Tomorrow belongs to the fluid and the multifaceted, Gerrold seems to be saying, and we ought to welcome, not condemn and persecute, them.

Easier said than done when fear is a natural reaction to what we find to be different from ourselves. If, indeed, we can't accept others at face value, how can we possibly know what to expect from those who are strange to us? How can we separate actual threats from encounters that could be harmless or even potentially beneficial? How can we hold on to our humanity when the Other can be such a frightening figure?

Maybe the best we can do—*should* do—is, like Slither, hold on to just enough of our souls—the parts that are most worthwhile—that we can survive any dangers that may arise and turn the face of the unknown into that of a friend, or even family.

During Slither's journey, they choose to befriend someone who's exactly such an unknown quantity. It's a conscious choice, one that in time means the difference between life and death.

Maybe, if all of us came to accept the Others we encounter, we might also be more heroic and able to strive for great things. If we were all more like Slither—without the killer instinct and cannibalism, perhaps—our own world might be a better and more hopeful place.

We might lack Slither's ability to shift our physical shapes, and our personal adventures might not be as exotic as theirs, but we might share the ability to reshape our own attitudes, and in so doing, to reshape destiny itself.

Then, whatever Spartans or tribbles or Sleestak we meet on our individual roads to the future, we may be more inclined to join forces than fight, finding the commonalities that enable us to mesh our infinite diversity in the compassionate combinations that are surely our truest and most rewarding final frontier.

—Robert Jeschonek

[1]Screenplay by Jean Lisette Aroeste, accessed online at http://www.chakoteya.net/StarTrek/ on March 6, 2025.

ONE

D idn't want the assignment, didn't like the assignment, refused to take the assignment, ended up with it anyway. The Old Man takes no for an answer like any other Italian grandmother. It's not in her vocabulary.

BTW, she's not an old man—at least, not this year, but that's only one of the things we call her. Partly because that's the job title and partly because she won't let us call her "mother" to her face . . . or the longer word of which "mother" is only the first two syllables.

I told her I wasn't going to take the job —I was overdue for leave and there was a very affectionate redhead waiting for me—but I never got that far. I got drafted instead, because I was the only one with the right physique. I'm five-five, mostly hairless, slender, and golden-dark. This month. Which means that even without makeup, even without much shifting, I can pass as a native almost anywhere—except perhaps Sweden.

Most folks think shifters are like amoebas —that we're boneless blobs of human gelatin, flowing into this shape or that like so much warm pudding poured into a mold. That's what comes from too much pop-life funneled into the brain. In truth, most shifting is makeup and acting and only a little bit of it is morphing. And the part that is morphing is mostly painful. I can shrink or stretch a couple of centimeters, and I can pump up with extra fluid and collagen if I have to, but the appearance of muscle isn't muscle, it's appearance.

A quick shift can be done in a week. A *real* shift can take six months or longer. This trip was an emergency, I'd be shifting in transit and onsite and I'd make up the difference with charm and a chador.

I like being female, even though it isn't my native gender. Mother says I have an aptitude. Three of my grandparents were shifters, both my parents were shifters, and my dad's eggs were sorted for Z-chromosomes before mom fertilized him, so there was never any doubt about my training. I grew up thinking that transformation was normal—and was shocked to find out that most human beings spend their whole lives in one identity and only the unhappy ones question why.

I have a repertoire of identities that I can drop into in a hurry. Depending on the makeup, I wake up an appropriate personality to the moment —but this was to be a quick wham-bam, rescue ma'am. In and out, by the book, catch you on the bounce, and all I needed to do was pass through customs. I'd go in as a naïve student. It sounded simple enough—which was why I refused. It's the simple ones that get people killed.

Mom refused to listen and tossed the mission file, a passport, and my tickets across the desk. "Your suitcase is packed, that's it by the door. Your makeup and a change of clothes are in the dressing room. You won't have time to change here, do it on the train. Your contact is Jiminy. Have a good trip. Be careful, I love you too, see you Thursday."

TWO

The train slid south out of Phoenix and I went to the dining car to carbo-load with as much bread and pasta as I could hold. I went through three cherry Cokes, and I pocketed all the sugar packets on the table too. Apple pie with ice cream for dessert, and on the way back to the cabin, I stopped at the snack bar and bought twenty dollars' worth of candy, pork rinds, Gatorade, and two cheeseburgers. It wasn't going to be enough, but I couldn't buy as much as I might need without calling attention to myself. I'd restock later, after the shift change.

Pulled the shades, hung a do-not-disturb, and locked the door. Stripped naked and took inventory. Not bad for a thirty-three-year-old man, but not very good for a twenty-two-year-old woman. Popped the appropriate pills and began the way I usually do, by massaging my nipples and my breasts—not because breasts are important, they are, but not the way most people think. But that's where I start getting into the mindset—by reminding myself that these things are sensory organs. Breasts are sensitive to temperature, sound, and physical well-being. Not to mention emotion. Most men think it's funny—I know I did the first time Mom told me to "listen with your tits." But most women know exactly what the experience is.

Mom taught me that being male is about projecting outward. It's about strength. And Dad said that being female is about listening inward. It's about assimilating and becoming. And that means being sensitive to the moment. What it means is being irritable. Look it up in the dictionary. Capable of responding to stimuli. In the case of a shifter, it means *abnormally* sensitive to stimuli. It also means easily annoyed, which is also accurate in my case.

Did I mention that shifting is painful? Not painful like screaming agony or burning needles, but painful like stretching the stiffness out, like working sore muscles, like pushing and stretching in six directions at once. But it's also very sensual. It's sexy. It's lustful. Part of the fun is standing in front of the mirror and modeling yourself into someone you want to fuck—or someone that other people want to fuck.

There's nothing wrong with being sexy. Unless of course, you're supposed to be inconspicuous, in which case, you have to go for *un*sexy. I usually try for sexy, but that's just because I want to see if I can still do it. The trick is to remember that sex isn't about sex, it's about sensuality.

Shifting to female is an internal/external process. Internal, you've got to shift gears from male-thinking to female—and that means a lot more than just letting go of the habits of testosterone. It means easing into a whole other geography of spirit. External—well, first there's that thing that makes men cross their legs in reflexive panic. You have to get rid of little Willy. Depending on whether it's a quick shift for appearances, or an in-depth shift for actual female function, the job can take anywhere from a few minutes to six weeks. For a quick shift, it's like inhaling a noodle, pulling everything up inside, and waiting for it to settle into a position that approaches comfortable. It's all there, if needed; it just doesn't show. This disturbs some men, it makes others curious—what does it feel like? It feels like what it feels like—kind of comfortable really, a much more sensible way to carry a particularly sensitive organ. A lot better than flopping around every which way in your panties.

The same time that's going on, there's a lot of fluid moving around upstairs and down. The body has to pump up the breasts and widen the hips. That means that the fat cells in the thighs and the butt and the stomach have to give up their fluid content, while the fat cells in the breasts and the hips absorb it. The waist shrinks, the figure curves. This process can be started in a few minutes, it takes about twelve hours to complete. It means frequent trips to the bathroom, and a lot of consumption of tea, milk, orange juice, soda, and aspirin.

And after all this has been started, then there's the depilatory. Begin with the body cream, belly, breasts, arms, underarms, neck, chin, back of the neck, shoulders, thighs, calves, pubis, gluteus maximus, anus, and then back to the belly again. Slowly and carefully. Three times. Remove all the body hair and awaken/stimulate/irritate the nerve endings. Finally finish with a damp towel, shove the residue into a plastic bag for discard. Massage the breasts again, listen with your tits. Feel for stubble. If you can feel any, do the whole thing again. That's the easy part. It's usually an hour or longer, by which time the first of the pills is kicking in.

When you're male, you let yourself get hairy, it helps the illusion. People see what they want to see. When you shift to female, you have to get rid of that hair and keep it from growing back—so the depilatory foam also contains hair retardants. I keep myself smooth with only a little bit of hair on my chest and a little bit more on my lower legs. That simplifies the shift to female, and when I go back to being male, I usually take on the appearance of a boy between the ages of fourteen and eighteen. If I need to appear older, I'm the wrong agent for the job.

Then there's the issue of underwear. I don't know why it's an issue, but it is. Some men absolutely refuse to wear women's underwear. Even when they're women. Which is why they're lousy shifters. And some men refuse to wear men's underwear, even when they're men, because women's underwear is more comfortable. Go figure. I just wear whatever the job requires, and at home I don't wear anything except a knee-length drape, the lightest possible material.

There's a price you pay for all this. Several prices. First, you're always body conscious. Not just body, but body-language too. Second, you're identity conscious. Am I being the right identity for this body? It's not an acting thing, it's a *being* thing.

And then there's the emotional price. Even if you wanted a lasting relationship, it's not going to happen. Most norms—and I mean that in the most derogatory sense possible—don't know how to have a relationship. They relate to bodies, to objects, to perceived identities—and the identities they project on each other. If your girlfriend turns into a boy as part of her job, that can be somewhat wilting. If your boyfriend turns into a girl, especially a pretty girl—well, some girls might find that exciting, but trust me, it really complicates everything. Mom says it takes two to entangle, but she's wrong. Even one person alone can make a world-class mess. Oh—and one more thing, the people who say they're turned on by shifters, stay away from them. A lot of them turn out to be weirdos. So most shifters stay within the family.

And finally, there's the physical price. It's exhausting. It's painful. It's draining. It ages you quickly. Even with the full-medical, even with the R&R, it's like being a champion athlete—you have to be in the gym every day, pushing yourself, stretching yourself, keeping yourself toned.

But I wouldn't have it any other way. Because I can do things, go places, and be all kinds of different people in all kinds of different situations. I get *insight*.

That's the real value of shifters. We *see* things.

We were well past Tucson and halfway to El Paso before I was done. I looked good. I'd even fuck me. But I skipped the makeup and draped myself in a poncho and baggy jeans and thick owlish glasses. I did not need the attention of the drunken cowboys who followed the southwest circuit. But I was still starving—

Another trip to the dining car and the snack bar and I'd be set for the night.

THREE

"You're a shifter, right?" He stopped me on my way back to my cabin.

"Huh?"

He was broad enough to block the entire passageway. A side of beef with a Texas accent and a grin so wide I'm surprised the top half of his head didn't fall off. Under other circumstances, he might be an evening of wonderful exercise. Tonight he was just in my way.

"No ordinary woman loads up like you do, hon—"

"I'm not your honey." I made as if to step past him. "If you'll excuse me—?"

He didn't take the hint. He tipped his hat and widened his smile, something I didn't think was possible. He nodded down at my armload of carbs and sugar. "If you need a little help burnin' off some those calories—" He hitched his pants meaningfully. Did he really just say that? I kept my face blank.

I frowned up at him. "Does that line ever

work?"

His eyes twinkled. "You'd be surprised." He turned sideways to let me pass. "I don't mean to intrude, but—well, yes I do. It's a long train ride and we're both a long way from home. I just thought we might make the ride a little easier—"

I slid past him. His chest was bigger than mine. He made it impossible for me to get past without me brushing my tits against him. He took it as an invitation.

"May I join you?"

"I'm not coming apart," I said. But he followed me down the corridor anyway. I tried to close my cabin door, but he pushed in behind me. That's when I knew I was going to have to kill him —

I almost didn't have the chance to act. He grabbed me from behind, one thick hand twisting my arm behind my back, the other across my mouth so I couldn't scream. I wouldn't have anyway, I had a better idea.

There's this that most people don't know about professional shifters—he didn't anyway— it's not all about shifting. I bit him. He didn't let go. It didn't matter. The drug took less than three seconds and he was out. I searched him, he wasn't carrying ID. I didn't think so. Contract killers rarely do.

Okay.

I shoved the pieces of his body out the train window. It's amazing what you can do with a good piece of razor-monofilament. With luck, the coyotes would find him and no one else would. But that was only the smallest part of the problem. Obviously, I'd been made. I'd have to abort. And that meant shifting again. Crap.

This was going to take all night, and it wasn't going to be fun. Or sexy. I'd just missed Deming, I'd have to get off at Las Cruces. I didn't dare risk going all the way to El Paso—

No, wait. I had a better idea.

San Antonio. Austin. New Orleans.

They'd be looking for me everywhere from Deming to Pecos. They'd assume I'd be off the train as fast as possible. But if I could stay aboard all the way to New Orleans, I could disappear into the Vampire Quarter.

Couldn't let Mom know. I trusted her. But if I'd been made, that might mean someone else couldn't be. There are ways to catch a mole, but I had a more immediate problem.

It's about survival—always have a Plan C, an escape hatch. Because Plan A is too obvious and Plan B is always desperate, except when it's the other way around.

So this tiny Mexican grandmother, Maria Hernandez, small and wrinkled, hobbling with a cane and a carpetbag, let herself out of the cabin at 4:30 in the ayem, when even the stewards were dozing, and found her way to the next-to-last car in the train, the cheapest seats possible, just in time to settle in next to a fat snoring businessman.

Grandma Hernandez had a bladder problem. She hobbled back to the lavatory at least once an hour, but by the time the train arrived at the Texican border, she was twelve kilos lighter and because of her stooped shoulders and bent knees 15 centimeters shorter. Her scraggly gray hair was pulled into a tight bun, accentuating the harshness of her bony features and squashed nose. Her teeth were terrible, rotting in her mouth. And she smelled bad. She hadn't bathed in days. She wasn't so repulsive as to draw attention to herself, just unkempt enough to be distasteful. You'd look away. That was the intention. Maria Hernandez had apparently boarded in El Paso, Texas. She had a ticket to New Orleans that she'd purchased from the onboard terminal. She'd paid in cash, a few dollars, mostly pesos.

Not a perfect cover, but there's no such thing as a perfect cover. There's only good enough. Any cover that takes a searcher's attention away from you is good enough.

I might not fool a trained professional, but people see what they think they're seeing. A shifter depends on it. Shifting is as much about perception as it is about shifting. I was counting on the black hats to be looking for a scrawny teenage boy or a petite little sexpot with nice tits. Those were the identities they thought they'd be looking for, but Maria Hernandez had never been seen in public before.

Dozing and cranky, she cussed out the conductor in some pretty astonishing *español* for waking her from her nap. But she passed over her ticket and passport anyway. He scanned it without comment, passed it back, and headed forward.

I slumped forward again, presumably back into Maria's exhausted nap. But more important, I was listening to the chatter on the line. Nothing about a missing Texican. Nothing about a missing female passenger either. That was weird, right there. Generally when someone goes missing, there's an alert. When two people go missing, it's 18 hours on the news cycle.

That was a bad sign. It meant there was a lid on it. And that meant—oh hell, it could mean anything, but most likely it meant that whoever was looking for me didn't want me to know they were looking for me. Or maybe it meant they did want me to know. They'd have to know by now that their assassin had failed. He would have reported immediately after completing his mission. His disappearance had to mean that he'd been killed instead. So now they knew that I knew that they knew that I was aboard. Unless I'd gotten off. It gets complicated.

It didn't matter.

It did, but it didn't. My need was to escape their surveillance net. If I knew where they were looking and who they were looking for, then I could put myself outside of the search area and be someone else entirely. But it's a lot more guesswork than most people want to believe. On both sides.

Despite what TV portrays, the one part that slows everything down is human beings. The right people have to be briefed, then they have to understand, then they have to make appropriate and rational decisions. And then—this is the good part—they have to hand off important parts of the job to underlings who, however well-trained they might be, will probably be much more mechanical than insightful in the performance of their duties. That's what I was depending on. The blindness of strangers.

And then the train slopped to a stop somewhere outside of a town so small, it's invisible from space. Black-armored troops in faceless helmets came striding into the car from both ends. *"Senora Hernandez. Ven con nosotros."*

"¿Por qué?" In my most tremulous voice.

It didn't work.

He was huge. They breed them for size—like bulls. Deliberate ultra-muscularity. He reached down and grabbed my arm and pulled me to my feet. Another guard grabbed my carpetbag.

Fighting was impossible. Biting wasn't an option. Neither was anything else in my arsenal. Not here. Too many innocents would be hurt or killed—and the outcome would be the same anyway.

They took me off the train. They handed me down to two more on the ground. Those two escorted me across a dusty dirt field. Behind us, the train growled off into the dawn.

I saw three black choppers squatting on the ground, bay doors open like mouths, blades lightly stropping the air. Another line of guards, matching the ones behind me. Too many. Escape not on the menu here.

"Strip it." That came from the one who must have been the commanding officer. He had a star on his helmet. No other marks.

The guards who'd taken me off the train now proceeded to remove my clothes. They wore heavy gloves and used garden shears to snip away each item. As each piece fell, they kicked it away. Another guard picked up each piece with hazmat tongs and dropped it into its own hazmat box. The guest of honor at a murder investigation didn't get such careful treatment.

Either this wasn't their first time, or they'd been training at this for a while. They were methodical and unembarrassed, taking their time with each step of the process. They finished with my filament-silk boxers. Damn, those were my favorite because they were the most comfortable. Those too disappeared into a hazmat box. Someday I'd smile at that, just not today.

Along the way, they recovered several slim-knives, two transmitters, both my poison-teeth, my earring cameras, the recording bracelet, my deadly little gold crucifix, and both my rings. The rest of the arsenal had been in my shoes, belt, purse, shawl, and padded bra.

I was left standing naked in the bright Texas morning, as alone as it was possible to be, in the center of a circle of guards—still Maria Hernandez —trembling, frightened, mumbling in Spanish, crying in confusion, trying to hide myself from their deadly gaze.

The guards ignored the performance.

What did they expect? That I would suddenly turn into a three-headed, fire-breathing dragon? Not hardly.

They went through my hair with gloved fingers, then sheared it off, leaving me with the barest stubble. They bent me over and probed my anus with something that buzzed and beeped, but wasn't much fun anyway. Another bent in front of me and used another device to explore my genital slit. They examined navel, armpits, ears, nose, mouth and throat. They took cheek swabs. They photographed my irises. They finished with a full-body scan—they rolled out a closet-sized unit. "Stand still." What was I going to do? Dance?

When it finished buzzing, they rolled it away.

As an afterthought, they placed my palms against a tablet-scanner and took my fingerprints. My footprints too.

Finally, the commanding officer came up to me. He looked me up and down. "If you're going to play an old lady, your tits should stretch to your navel."

He was right. I hadn't had time. Maria Hernandez still had the breasts of a teenage girl. Or a teenage boy fooling around at the hormone counter. Maybe there are flat-chested old ladies, or even perky-boobed septuagenarians—especially with modern science—but that wasn't Maria Hernandez.

Another guard came up to him and showed him the display on a tablet. He nodded. My guess—the scan had revealed several implanted microchips.

"Spray it," he ordered. The "it" was deliberate. A shallow attempt to deprive me of masculine or feminine identity, the first step in breaking me down. It didn't work. I've been called worse. My identity isn't based on other people's opinions. If it were, I could never have been a shifter.

A couple of black guards came up, carrying things that looked like fire-extinguishers. They sprayed me up and down with chalk-smelling foam. It hardened quickly into a complete body shell. A plastic cocoon. Vaguely translucent. I took a deep breath and closed my eyes when they sprayed around my head. They left my face clear, but slapped a blank mask in place so I couldn't see or speak. Not that I was going to say anything anyway. I could still see and hear through my skin, not clearly, but enough to have a sense of location.

Then they did some other stuff—I couldn't tell from the inside, but logically they must have been spraying some additional coats of blocking material on the cocoon to prevent any signals in or out to my tracking chips. Whoever they were, they were good. After everything had hardened, they put me on something with wheels and rolled me away, finally up a ramp, and into a darker, quieter space that vibrated. After a moment, we lifted up and away.

There's this about being taken. Your captors are going to want information. But how they behave, what they say, what they do, what they ask, they're going to give up a lot of information about themselves in the process.

Already I knew three things. 1) They were well-organized. They had to be to execute an operation like this. 2) They had resources— choppers, technology, personnel. 3) Our security was compromised. They had made me from the beginning.

And 4) They were ruthless. They had sent an assassin after me.

Wait a minute—I had presumed he was an assassin. Perhaps he wasn't. Perhaps his mission had simply been acquisition and extraction.

Because if they wanted me dead, why go to all this trouble to immobilize and transport me?

Probably because I'd already demonstrated that I didn't want to be acquired and extracted.

Okay, maybe they weren't that ruthless. Maybe they wanted something else?

Information? But if they knew who I was and where to find me, then what information could I possibly have that they didn't already have?

5) I could estimate my approximate location by how long we were in the air. Less than an hour. Assume we're not crossing the border south into Mexico. The Republic of Texas does not have good relations with its unhappy neighbors to the south. Or north. Or west for that matter. They weren't the best neighbors to have anyway. So, most likely, we were heading northeast, probably to one of the installations south of Dallas.

So rescue was out of the question. Mom wouldn't invade a foreign country, couldn't risk international repercussions. The Texicans were fussy that way.

Escape?

Not bloody likely.

If they were going to this much trouble to capture and hold me, then whatever containment they intended for me would certainly be even more secure.

Reviewed my options. There weren't any. Wait and see.

After landing, they rolled me across concrete, up a ramp, into an elevator, down at least four levels, through a series of halls and doors, into a lab so bright I could sense the difference through the mask across my face.

Something hissed. After a moment, I began to feel fuzzy and relaxed. Something else buzzed. I felt warm and bright for a few seconds. A little later, something clanged and clattered loudly.

If they were who I thought they were, then I had been scanned up and down the entire spectrum, given a time-locked 3D X-ray, explored with polarized magnetic resonance, bio-thermal imaged, microwave mapped, and rotisserie-digitized. They now knew where every one of my implants and biochips were located. If they were curious, they would remove them for study—if not, then they'd simply disable them with targeted EMPs.

Finally, they moved me to a very small, very quiet place. I could tell by the difference in the sound. More hissing. They were spraying the cast of hardened foam that held me immobile. More hissing and I went dark.

Came awake with someone spraying me, stinging hot water. The hose played up and down my skin. A pressure-wash. Blinked up into the light. Everything still a blur.

"Don't talk." A male voice.

Hadn't been planning to. I couldn't see him clearly. I didn't try to move. Wasn't sure how long I'd been out or what drugs they might have used. When in doubt, be limp, save energy. He lifted various straps to wash beneath them. When he let go, they tightened again. I wasn't going anywhere.

Another stinging spray, this time hot air and hot light. He lifted the straps one by one and dried me methodically, dispassionately. When he was finished, he draped a micro-silk sheet over me. Unnecessary, I can regulate my own internal heat. But again, more useful information. These people did not know everything. They did not know half of what they were dealing with.

The question wasn't whether I could escape. The question was how long it would take and how many I would have to kill. There were still a few things that their machines should not have detected.

The problem was energy debt.

I didn't have a lot of fat to burn. Certainly

not enough for a prolonged assault. I'd have to replenish. There would be protein available after I killed a few of them—especially the ultra-musculars. But that would leave a bad taste in my mouth, metaphorically.

On the plus side, the discovery of a half-eaten bull would unnerve the entire facility while I was dormant and recharging. But it would make the next steps even more difficult.

I could wait.

I'd missed three check-ins. Mom would have scrambled, locked-down, and burrowed—all the separate pieces isolated and cell-blocked. In plain Spanglish, Mom and the family no longer existed.

There was another possibility. A nastier one. But I wasn't ready to go there. I'd have to ride this one to the end and see what was in the gift shop.

Behind me, a door closed with a soft hushing sound. The straps around my wrists and ankles eased. The wider heavier straps across my chest and waist and thighs also relaxed. A moment later, they released and retracted. I was free to sit up. If I felt like it. I didn't. There was no point.

I waited.

Considered the possibilities.

They were probably thinking they could break me. The first part of the process would be isolation. Time deprivation. Time distortion. Interrupted sleep cycles, disrupted eating cycles.

Six weeks at least.

And then how many more months of sensory assault? Loud unpleasant noises. Hyper-music. Bright flashing lights, designed to trigger seizures. Hallucinatory imagery projected on the walls. Interrupted by lengthy periods of total silence and darkness.

I didn't feel like wasting my time, but I'd stay for a while—long enough to learn a little. Long enough to learn how advanced they were. Or weren't.

A soft voice came from an overhead speaker. Possibly male, more likely female. Maybe something in-between. Hard to say. Dusky, low, neutral—appropriately dispassionate.

"This is unfortunate."

I thought about possible responses. All of them ended with a question mark. I said nothing.

"You do understand why this is unfortunate, don't you?"

This could go six different ways. I remained inert, but alert.

"We can make your time here very unpleasant. We could spend months exposing you to a wide variety of disruptive stimuli. But it wouldn't work. You know that. We know that. It would waste our time and resources. It would produce little or no useful result. And it would give you information about our abilities that we would prefer not to reveal."

Hmm. That was an interesting sentence. He—she?—had just admitted something. Maybe weakness, maybe strength—maybe fear. Hard to say. But it was a data point.

"It's all right. You don't have to speak. We can still monitor your responses. You're very good at keeping yourself inert."

Might as well relax then.

"Thank you." Was there a hint of a smile in that voice? "So if interrogation is no longer useful, then we have to look at our other options. We could terminate you..."

Yes, you could.

"—but that would also be counterproductive. Your organs might contain embedded microspores that would be released in any subsequent dissection. You might have other undetectable self-destruct or doomsday devices within your body. Even a sputtered tracking signal could expose ourselves and our facilities."

I allowed myself a smile, I just didn't let it show on my face. Whoever these people were, they were smart, cautious, methodical, and thoughtful. They had also just revealed some of the limitations of their ability to counter.

"So that option has to be discarded. We entomb you. We could put you at the bottom of a well and fill it with concrete. Or we could flashburn you. Or drop you into the Marianas Trench. But any of those disposal methods might attract the attention of others."

Click. Another piece of the puzzle.

Mom—or someone in the office—would have been tracking the train. The security drones cruising 20 kilometers up would have provided visual recon. Mom would have seen the train stopped, she would have seen the arrest of Maria Hernandez. She would have tracked the chopper to its landing. I had been transferred from the chopper directly to the elevator. No truck or ambulance between.

Therefore...

Possibilities piled up.

It could be a facility on the edge of an airport, a front of some kind, everything paid through double-blind dummies. But no, if you've invested in that kind of front, you don't want to give it up that easily. Unless it was deliberately created to be given up. Hm.

Or maybe this was someplace else, some remote station in the middle of the wastelands. Some place you don't use, don't care about, and don't mind giving up. A clean site, firewalled, with no hardwired connections.

Still processing—Mom had to have tracked the chopper, so she must have a pretty good idea where I am. She'd have to be moving SCRAM teams onto the perimeter. That would explain why my captors had no time for a prolonged interrogation.

Or...we were so deep into Texas that assembling and moving a SCRAM team was a logistical nightmare. Not impossible, just time-consuming. We were a long way from the California Archipelagoes.

The owner of the voice had to be aware of that as well.

Either way, the clock was running.

"I see you're working it out. We cannot safely dispose of you without risking detection." A long thoughtful pause. Then the voice continued, "We could contain you, immobilize you with drugs or other measures that would take you out of the game. That's also an option. But not cost-effective. It would require an investment of effort on our part to keep you contained and that would use up resources better spent elsewhere. And whether you want to acknowledge this or not, it would not significantly hinder the operations of those who sent you."

Hmm. That was an interesting sentence too.

"So. We really have only one option...."

I waited.

Silence.

Ah ha.

Nice.

There are two kinds of people in the world: Those who need closure.

Nothing happened for a long time. Then something hissed and the air smelled like lime. I went out.

FOUR

The cold woke me up.

I rolled over and stared at the sky. Stars—very bright stars.

This was almost comfortable. A cool breeze rustled over me. The ground beneath me was firm where it needed to be, soft where I wanted it. Nice view—

Wait—

Stars?

Night?

Outside?

Right.

Groggy.

But automatic reflexes kicked in anyway.

Deep breath. Another. A third.

Inventory? All here?

Coming awake. Coming active.

Still groggy. It'll pass.

Finally. Stand up. Look around.

Desert.

Hard to make things out in just the starlight, but I've got a couple advantages. Just a matter of adjusting the eyes.

Low scrub. Scattered Joshua-looking things. A few round bushes that might someday be tumbleweeds.

And a very faint hint of light beneath the horizon.

Oh, and I'm naked. Nice touch. Very nice. The cold wind reminded me of that. My bare skin prickled. I could adjust. Consciousness expanded. Oddly silent. No transmissions in or out.

Had to get my bearings. Turned slowly, looking for landmarks. Anything. The night was moonless. The stars were unnaturally bright. And I felt weird. An after-effect of the drug? Most likely.

I'd have to think about that—after my head cleared. The cold air was helping. I couldn't smell any telltales, but I wasn't that familiar with Texas anyway. Not my favorite place on the planet.

Where the hell was I? Probably far enough from the site that I couldn't find my way back to it. If there were any tracks on the ground, I didn't see them in the dark. Not even heat signatures. I'd probably been choppered here and dropped.

Yes, dropped. I had scrapes and bruises.

Nothing serious broken. They must have flown low to avoid detection. Soft enough ground. Hard enough body. Either they didn't understand or they didn't care.

A thought was forming, somewhere deep down.

That light on the horizon. Had to be the closest approximation of civilization. But friendly? Not necessarily. Thought about heading toward it. Probably not the smartest idea, but definitely the least stupid. I'd have to pick my way carefully. Not used to bare feet and I didn't want to step on something nasty. Like a scorpion. Or a rattlesnake. Or fire ants. That would ruin my whole day. I decided to sit and think.

Anyway...now I knew what the third option was.

They couldn't get information out of me, they were too cautious to risk killing me. All that was left was to—very smart—neutralize my effectiveness.

Maybe they'd tagged me somehow and I was being tracked. Whenever I managed to reconnect, they'd have an access.

So...I couldn't reconnect. Not without risk to the family. Clever. Very clever. They'd neutralized me. Mom would never know. Well, not quite. There were a few blind drops I could use to let her know what had happened. But Mom wouldn't—couldn't—reach out. I was pretty much on my own. If I was tagged and tracked, and I had to assume I was, then I was effectively retired.

Maybe. Probably. There was no way to know. So I had to stay out in the cold.

Literally.

The night was starting to bite. This was not going to be fun.

Okay, stop.

Deep breath. Calm down. Stamp your feet and shiver. Do the homeostasis thing. Another deep breath. Look at the sky and take your bearings—

The sky—

I stared, turned, stared some more, then slowly began to figure it out. A sick sinking feeling that started in my throat, fell through my chest, dropped through my gut and left me so weak in the knees, I collapsed to the ground weeping.

I didn't recognize any of the constellations in the sky. Neither did my augments. Deep search. Deeper. Nothing.

Now I knew where I wasn't.

They'd pushed me through a portal—I was off-planet. Unknowable light years distant. I bounced a few times, testing. Right. A smidge less than one gee. I hadn't noticed. I'd been too foggy, too confused—

I started screaming. Cursing. A torrent of obscenities in six different languages, including Shakespearean English.

Oh, you foul-smelling pustules, you pox-laden whelps, you unmuzzled elf-skinned flap-dragons, you pribbling fly-bitten scullions, you ruttish, bat-fowling, leather-jerking, crystal-bottom, knot-pated, agattering, puke-stocking, caddis-garter, smooth-tongue varlots—

That cleared my head nicely. And warmed me up a bit. Me and Willy. Mostly Willy. But he's dead and Ghu knows how many light years away, so he can't complain about the collaboration.

I'm good for thirty seconds of anger. That's all I need. After that, it's just drama. A waste of time and energy.

And besides, it's not very ladylike.

But there was also that other thing.

Whatever it was, out there watching me.

I'd been aware of it for a while.

So far, it was just watching, maybe wondering if I'd be good to eat. I could hear it breathing.

But now I could hear it shifting its weight, calibrating its stance for a sudden charge.

Not sure what it was. Didn't recognize the breathing. Cat? Wolf? Bear? Something modified? Or something native to this world? That was another question. Alien ecology or terraformed? I'd worry about that later.

The thing charged.

It wasn't a fair fight. The poor thing never had a chance.

I went into hyper-speed, not enough to turn the world into slo-mo, I didn't want a total energy debt, just enough to assess its weaknesses, shift my position, and slice its belly open to pull out its intestines. Did I forget to mention I had claws? Not long, but long enough and sharp enough.

I don't like eating meat raw. It's too tough. But it's better than starving, it analyzed as protein and protein is fuel. This was good enough to feed my considerable energy debt, but not much more than that. But time spent chewing is also a good time for thinking—for a person who can split their brain into multiple processes, that is. So I chewed and I thought.

It wasn't reassuring.

The first thought—I had been dropped here to die.

But the black-hats who'd delivered the goods had made an unfatal assumption. They'd given me a triple dose of sleepy-time and assumed it would be enough to either kill me or keep me comatose long enough to ship me out and drop me where the local wildlife could have an easy lunch. And no remains would ever be found.

Fair enough. It made sense from their point of view.

It would have worked on any other human being.

What they didn't know, couldn't know, was just how much I had been augmented. I had enough interior hardware that I was somewhere on the other side of trans-human. My augments weren't just hardened and muted, they were organic. Non-metallic. Nothing would have shown up on a standard scan. They gave me sleepy-time and I went into hibernate mode, my autonomics only awakening enough to start neutralizing the bad stuff circulating in what passed for my blood stream.

So I woke up.

They screwed up.

I wasn't supposed to recover consciousness.

But I did, and I ate.

I can't say it tasted good. It didn't. But it was useful protein and I needed to bulk up with a few layers of fat. The night was getting colder and I had no idea how long until dawn.

FIVE

S o while I waited to finish waking up—
there was a lot of me to bring back
online and it had to be done in the right sequence
—I sat and thought.

Someone had shoved me into a portal—
through a series of portals, because none of
the portals were one-stop. Getting from Earth
to anywhere required multiple portal jumps. It
had something to do with local safety issues
(since the Montana blow-out) and the much more
complicated job of punching a hole through space.
Whatever. Maybe someone else can explain it. I'm
not a quantum mechanic.

Whoever had dropped me here had not
come themselves, not needed to. Life-supporting
worlds are always one-way trips. The quarantines
are total. No risk of biological contamination can
be allowed to return to Earth.

So I was drugged, packed, and shipped to
someone who was willing to accept receipt of the
package and deliver the contents as specified in the
manifest. Drop the body somewhere in the desert.

Maybe it wasn't a colleague of the 'voice.' Maybe just a paid expediter. Either way, not a friendly.

They couldn't kill me on Earth. My death would have triggered all sorts of alarms, tracking devices, and possibly a few internal explosives. They couldn't know. But they had to neutralize me somehow. Considering the multiple potential threats that I might represent, offworld removal of not-yet-dead operator was probably the most expedient.

They had succeeded. I had to give them points for that.

Well, almost.

I didn't die.

But either way, I'm no longer a threat to anything on Earth.

Who were they? Dunno. One truth about the universe, there will never be a shortage of enemies. We can have shortages of everything else, truth, justice, equality—but never a shortage of people who've decided to hate someone else. Sometimes they're even justified. But mostly not.

Process of elimination, it wasn't the Texicans. They weren't advanced enough. It had to be someone else, some outside agency—operating either with or without the Texicans' knowledge and/or approval.

Whoever it was, they had to know what they were doing.

Well almost.

I didn't die.

That was useful information too. They knew a lot. They just didn't know enough.

What else?

Mom had insisted the mission was urgent. Had they fooled Mom? That was unlikely. Or had Mom's own security been compromised? Did Mom have a mole? That was even more unlikely. But if not, then had Mom set me up? That didn't make sense either.

And then there was that last ugly thing. I had screwed up. Badly. I had passed up six opportunities to escape, but I'd kept telling myself that we needed to know who they were so I waited to discover and unfortunately I waited too long.

That was the harder question. Was this the real mission Mom wanted me to go on? Go out and get captured? Find out who and what and why?

She had to know it was a setup. Mom wasn't stupid.

But after all that, it just didn't matter.

I was here. They were there. And I had more immediate problems to deal with.

SIX

I like the idea of survival. I'm biased that way. Maybe it's just a bad habit, but after so many years of practice I'm used to it.

So ...

Did I know this world? There wasn't much in my database. It had to be one of the unlisted ones. There were too many corporations opening offworld portals. They weren't reporting their successes, only their failures. Successes were taxable. Failures were deductible.

So. Secrets. Somewhere down the line, up the line, off the line, here I was and I had only two real questions to consider. How long was night on this planet and what was that very faint glow on the horizon ... ?

I would find out the length of the night on this world soon enough. All I had to do was wait. The other question, however ...

What kind of station or installation was it? I couldn't assume they'd be happy to see me. These were probably the people who had dropped me in the desert, who couldn't be bothered to take me far enough over the horizon that I wouldn't see the glow of their settlement—unless they took me far enough that I would see the lights of some other installation.

Why would they drop me close enough to see the lights? Close enough to come back? Or maybe it's just something that the chopper crew didn't notice. Or didn't care about. Or maybe they knew it was there and the location was intentional—

Yes, I do overthink things.

Oh, silly me. I was looking with my eyes. I could see the glow. They couldn't. So they had obviously assumed they were far enough out. Right.

So, next question. What's out there? And who? I don't even know what planet I'm on. There are several hundred known portal worlds, most of them useless except for occasional mining, and at least twice that many more that haven't been registered.

But only a few are shirtsleeve worlds. So where am I and what's over there? What kind of situation am I walking into?

Do I need to be male or female—and how old? What color? What language will I need to speak? And do I have enough energy to shift?

Some of the portal worlds had been

colonized by religious or ethnic minorities—not to mention ideological settlements and gender-based communities. I doubted very much that I'd been dropped on Haven, Paradise, or Shangri-La.

More likely—

Oh, shit.

—at least three of the portal worlds had been set aside for hardened criminals, gangs, and psychopaths. It was occasionally convenient to shove political prisoners and other unpleasant loose ends into those particular portals. Especially if you had no qualms. Especially if it gave you a gleeful sense of gotcha. Coventry.

It could be very dangerous for me to approach any semblance of what passed for civilization here. It all depended on how sadistic or angry my captors had been. After all, I had killed one of their agents.

I had options.

Obviously, I could just walk into town and hope for the best.

Or I could sneak up to the edge of whatever settlement and try to observe until I could figure out a safe course of action.

Or I could just walk up to the least hostile-looking door and knock. "Hello, sorry to trouble you. Can you tell me where I am?"

I doubted I could get that close without

detection. Whoever they might be, they'd probably have a security net. And that's another question. Just what kind of apex predators inhabit this planet? The one I was feasting on might have been a local opportunist. There were likely others, bigger and uglier.

I hadn't heard any howling or roaring or yipping—and that was even worse news. A fresh kill has a downwind presence, a spreading invitation to buzzards, jackals, hyenas, and various species of cat-things, whatever filled the same ecological niches on this planet.

A stalking predator doesn't announce itself by roaring. It also doesn't stop to roar after it brings down the prey. It keeps a strangle hold on the windpipe until the prey not only stops struggling, but its heart stops beating as well. And by then, the predator is too exhausted to roar. It has to catch its breath and then decide whether or not to eat or drag the kill back to its den or up a tree or into a gully so other predators won't find it.

There weren't a lot of predators left on Earth. They hadn't survived the eco-collapse. But all the documentaries about the animals from before were still fascinating. They were part of the training—because to be effective in my skills, I had to learn how to think like a predator. The bad news was that even apex predators failed to make a kill three times out of four.

As a trained operator, I had to be better than

that.

Maybe I smell so alien to the predators on this planet, they might not want to approach. But the thing whose leg I was munching on right now hadn't thought so.

I might have something else stalking me through the darkness at this very moment. And I, in my clumsy roughshod way, would have no way of knowing what to listen for. I stopped, sniffed, listened, peered, tasted the wind. Even with my enhancements, I couldn't detect anything out of the ordinary—because now that I was sniffing and listening and squinting and tasting, *everything* was out of the ordinary. I'm not stupid. I dragged what was left of my lunch—dinner?—found a defensible hollow and hunkered down in it to wait for sunrise.

The stars turned slowly.

Too slowly.

But it was still useful. I now had a sense of direction. That glow beyond the horizon was east.

Except I had no idea when sunrise would occur. How long was the night on this planet? And when had I been dropped? Twilight? Midnight? Near dawn?

No, not near dawn. Or I would have seen a little more glow in the east.

I couldn't afford to hunker down and wait. What if the night on this world was 36 hours long?

By midnight, the temperature would be below freezing. Maybe that was part of their plan too. Not knowing how to safely terminate me, they'd put me in a non-survivable situation. Even with my augments, I might be dead of exposure before morning. Already I could feel the chill as a deeper bite.

I had to get moving.

But that brought me to another question. What was their intention in dropping me here? I mean *here*.

Why am I still alive? They could have just as easily shoved me through a portal where nothing could live. One of the black vacuum places. Why this place? If they were going to send me to a habitable world, they wouldn't drop me someplace where death was inevitable. Was this a test to see what I could survive? That didn't make sense either. My best guess was that whoever they were, they were probably stupid or clumsy or lazy. Or all three. Or some deeper motive that I still hadn't sussed out. That was possible. Internal monitoring said I was still feeling the after-effects of the drugs.

Ah, the penalties of having an overactive mind. I can worry about six impossible things before second breakfast.

And that was another one. Food. I had no idea what might be the effects of the protein I had just consumed. I needed it, and I had enough internal safety mechanisms that even three-day carrion wouldn't kill me. But…on the other hand, there was that old saying, "What you don't know that you don't know—that shit can kill you."

"Shut up," I said. "You're over-thinking it again."

On the other hand, over-thinking had kept me alive this far.

Never mind. I started walking.

The glow was brighter now. That was odd—

And then it burst over the horizon and it was too bright. Brighter than daylight. The whole landscape lit up with stark shadows hurled sideways into a world of sudden twilight. I held up my hands against the harrowing glare. My skin was transparent, I could see my bones, I had to turn away. I dialed it down, but it was still an overload.

And even more lights now—

—circling overhead. Blazing fingers stabbing from the sky, bright ovals tracing back and forth across the ground, then closing and pinning me where I stood—caught in a silent firestorm of actinic brilliance, a wash of luminosity so intense it penetrated the flesh.

Despite the howling glare, my mind was racing. How long had those drones been tracking me through the dark? Tried to recap. Someone had been watching me on the monitors. What had I given away?

Turned away from the light in self-defense. If they were going to shoot me, they would have done it already. Around me, multiple shadows bounced and shuddered. Finally, I heard the crunch of tires on dirt. High beams and even more spotlights targeted me where I stood. The wall of dazzlement made it possible to see through my own hands and arms, I was a skinny squinting toothpick skeleton, outlined with a dozen flickering shadows.

I had maybe three seconds to decide—

Paralyzed, trembling, I collapsed in fear. And hoped they'd buy it. Added some realistic sobs—gasped for breath as well. Maybe the drones hadn't seen me killing and eating that wolf-thing.

Footsteps across the dirt. Someone talking to a phone. "It's a li'l boy, pa. Nekkid. Can y' see'm? Yah. No. Hell'f I know. Nah, he don' look dangerous. Scared as shit-fuck. No prob. Yah, I'll bring 'm. Yah. Mac out."

Click, click, tap, tap. "Aerial Team B, return to patrol. Ground Team Team B, stand down, return to base."

Half of the overheads went out. Then half of the ground vehicles dimmed and pulled away. I still couldn't see. Still too bright. I could barely make out a silhouette. He wore armor, a helmet, goggles, a face mask. He wore a battery pack and pointed a no-bullshit railgun. He lowered the weapon, but there must have been others still pointed at me, behind the lights.

"C'n you git up?" Strange accent. Couldn't identify it. Might have been a slurried form of east Texas. "Y'need hand? There any more o' y' out there? How'd y' get out here, anywhy? Who are y'?"

Managed to shake my head, still sobbing, lifted a hand for him to help me up. Held the other hand to cover my sex. If he thought I was a boy, I'd better be one. Started cobbling an identity— maybe.

He seized my wrist. He was tall and gangly, but he wasn't weak. He half-walked, half-dragged me to an oversized vehicle, a giant pill-shaped beast on monster wheels. Racks of spotlights, front and back. Two weapons turrets. Cameras, antennas, radar as well. A quick glimpse of the others still here—just as big, just as well equipped, but apparently uninhabited. Maybe. Not sure. But probably. Bots. Drones. Whatever. A private little army. Whoever these people were, they were ready for battle. So now I had a new question. Who else or what else might be out here in the desert? What had I escaped from? And what had I escaped into?

He pushed me up a steep ladder, through a hatch in the upper level and into the back of the vehicle. It was more luxurious than I expected. He climbed up front and fiddled with his controls for a bit. Some of the lights around us dimmed, then shifted. The other vehicles were moving away. Ours shuddered to life and followed.

After a bit, he must have been satisfied that the autopilot was managing. He pulled off his helmet and came back to examine me. The armor gave him a bulky look, but it hung loose on him. It looked scorched and well-used. Scratches and patches. By then, I had managed to squeeze out something that might look like a very small, very cold penis. Beans and frank.

I was still shivering. Deliberately. He opened an overhead bin and pulled out a blanket, something like wool, and tossed it over. I let it fall to the floor. He picked it up and wrapped it around me. It was scratchy. Reckless move on his part. Because now I had a sense of his strength. I could take him. If I had to.

"Y' got a name?" he asked.

Shook my head. Still trembling.

"'kay. Don't need one out here, nevva'min'. Just call y' 'hey there' f'now. Hang in for a bit, we'll git y' warmed." He stepped past me, fiddled in the galley, came back with a thermal-mug, popped the top. Hot broth of some kind. Beef? Way out here? Hard to tell what was in it. Curious under-taste. Unfamiliar. Had to trust it anyway.

"Now y' drink that and git cozy. I got work up front. Gotta check, make sure the perimeter's secure. Probly is. But y' never know." He patted my leg. Not entirely a reassuring pat, his hand slid a bit. He was either patting me down or checking me out. Hard to say. I squinted after him, still not breaking character. Under all that gear he might be cute. Or not. Maybe the penis was premature? No. Not gonna risk a rape either. Then I'd have to kill him. That one's a personal rule. It goes all the way back to the day that pig-faced Tommy and squint-eyed Harold pushed me up against the lockers and tried to feel me up—I got expelled. They got a trip to the emergency room.

I scrooched myself up into a sitting position, cupped the mug with both hands, unsealed the lid, and sipped carefully. Was it drugged? Probably not, but by now I'd been in and out too often to be sure. If it was, I still had to drink it to stay in character.

Opened my ears to listen to the chatter. He seemed to be talking to one person only. Pa. Everything else was bots and drones. He was monitoring several areas at once. The front of the vehicle was wide-curved display, lit up with maps, schematics, thermal images, and visuals from several hundred stereo-cameras, flickering in and out at a dizzying pace, the view pausing only if something was actively moving within the locus of inspection—usually another vehicle or drone.

Finally, he came back. He'd loosened his armor to be more comfortable, but he still didn't trust me.

"Feelin' better? Y' are? My name's Mac.

What's y'rs?"

I grunted something unintelligible.

"Yah. Lotta people got that name. Now, y' wanna tell me how you got y'rself dropped out here? Who'd you piss off?"

Shook my head. The more questions he asked, the more I would know what to answer.

He put his hand on my forehead, tilted my head back, peered into my eyes. I kept my expression blank. "Yah. Y'r still in shock." He turned my face from side to side. "Kinda pretty f'r a boy. Might keep y'." He said it with a smile, then he let go and got serious again. "Ain't no dokkers this side. Most of 'em stay close to the portal. They won't come out this far. But if y' ain't got no broken bones, or internal injuries, we c'n get you warmed up back at the station. Med unit there'll check y' out."

I might be able to pass a low-tech med-scan, but if it was military grade, he'd know I was a slither. I'd have to recover enough to make it unnecessary.

Blinked my eyes, pushed my hair back off my forehead, managed a weak smile. "Thankie."

"Ah, It speaks." He grinned. "Who are y' now? How'd y' get here? We had a chopper cross the northeast sectern a few hours back. They drop you? Why?"

"Dunno why." I had my story ready. It would

be a hard one to check. Almost believable. In my best trembling adolescent voice, "M'name is Billy Jule. My dad is a monitor in New Mexico—"

"Where's New Mexico.? Never heard of it—"

"You never heard of New Mexico? It's right between Arizona and Texas—"

"Ah, yah. There's the problem. Y'r on Sparta, little'un."

"Sparta? Where's Sparta? Is that in Texas?"

"No, little'un. It isn't."

"But—how'd I get here?"

"Whyn't you tell me?"

"Um, please? I just want to go home—" I blurted it out like a frightened tweener. "I was on my way home. From school. But some men grabbed me at the train station. And—and they put a hood over my head. They took my phone and my tablet and I think they scrambled my locater chip or burned it out or something. Because nobody came for me. They kept me locked up in a room somewhere. Foil on all the walls and windows. It was like some kind of a jail or something. Then they said that my dad wouldn't pay for me, I guess they thought he was rich. I thought they were going to kill me—"

"No. They sold you, little'un. They sold you to—well, it doesn't matter. But we get a lot of drop-offs."

"So...I'm going to be all right then? You're going to send me back?"

"Wish I could. But I can't." He put his hand on my leg again. Firmly. And added what he must have thought was a reassuring smile. His hand slid toward my thigh, but not too far. Not foreplay yet.

"See, here's the thing, little'un. This's a one-way ticket. We're twelve portals out from Earth. About as far as you can get. They must've had you in deep storage. It's a long, long ride, even on a fast train. It's a good place to hide, an even better place to get lost. But you can breathe the air and drink the water, so that's got to be good for somethin'."

Had to sound very uncertain now. "What do you mean, one-way ticket?"

"I mean you ain't goin' home again. This is it."

"But—but—you have to send me back—"

"Little'un, you'd have to break at least three-four quarantines between here and there. And that's not happenin'. Ever. Last coupla guys who tried it—they burned 'em on the spot."

So I started weeping. I might even have meant it.

Mac looked distressed. He took off his helmet and rubbed his hand through his hair. It was short and bristly and kind of sandy colored. He looked toward the front of the vehicle, then back to me. He looked annoyed, confused, frustrated.

"Well now, here's ta other thing, little'un. You and me, we got a bigger problem. See— there ain't no girls allowed here. On Sparta. It's a monoculture. All male."

"I'm not—"

"Yah. Y' are. Don't try and fun me. I only look stupid."

Oh, crap. Was I going to have to kill him now? I didn't want to. He was kind of cute—

"I saw y' before you covered yourself with your hand. There weren't nothin' there. I think somebody played a real nasty trick on you, little'un."

I tried to be impassive. Right. There is no try. I think, this time, some of my feelings might have shown. And the worst wasn't over.

"And uh, by the way—that Billy Jule story, it's a good 'un too, but it ain't gonna sell. Not here. So whoever y' are and however y' got here—we got a problem. And we don't have a lot of time to figger it out. I mean, right now, it's just me and Pa running this stretch. But the monitors are gonna start askin' questions about you, just as soon as dawn cracks. We got mebbe another thirty hours. So now, let's you and me stop wasting each other's time. Cut the crap and we'll start over. Otherwise, I'll have to tell 'em y' died in transit. And neither one of us is gonna like that very much. But there'll be a lot less questions to answer. For me, the only important one will be, 'did you burn it before you buried it, or do we gotta detox the ground?' Now…" He stared into my face. "Let's start with y'r real name. Y' got one?"

I took a breath. I didn't remember. I'd had so many names. "Just call me Slither."

"Slither. Is that y'r birth name?"

I shook my head. "It's all I got. It's not a name. It's a—a job description."

"Well that's a start." He sat down opposite me, relaxed. Sort of. He still had one hand loosely by his side—where a flat pistol rode. In my present condition, I wasn't going to risk it.

"Okay, what's a slither? What are y'?"

I finished the last of the broth and put the cup aside. "I'm a—well, I was—a courier. I deliver things. Mostly information. Things that need to be moved from one place to another."

"A smuggler?"

"Might say it that way."

"Hm," he said. "Might have use for a smuggler." Then he peered harshly at me and shook his head. "But y' wouldn't work here. Little'uns usually stay close to home."

I can bulk up well, but I didn't say that aloud. Not giving up any more information than I have to. Doing it right would take too long anyway.

"So, who'd y' piss off?"

"Dunno. They didn't give their names."

"Doesn't matter anyway. They're not here. Y' are." He rubbed his hand through his hair again. "Big question, what do I do with y'…? Y' ever work as a bed-warmer?"

Nothing I want to discuss, no. Aloud, "What's a bed-warmer?"

"Well, see—" He took a deep breath. "Nobody pays too much attention to them. Might could hide y' that way for a bit. Nobody asks about a bed-warmer."

I must have given away my reaction. I was tired enough. Because he said, "Indentures. Some boys can't afford a ticket. They sell seven years. We train 'em, they end up with a set of skills. And if they're valuable enough to keep around, sometimes even a share of the household. I can tell Pa you're a lost little'un and we're good. Pa ain't gonna ask, he don' care. If no one shows up to claim your contract, we write our own. Not likely anyone's gonna come lookin' for y'."

I held myself impassive. The way Mac told it, I didn't have a lot of options here. If he was telling the truth. I had no reason to doubt him. He wasn't giving off any "I'm a goddamn liar" signals. Except for that business with his too-friendly hand on my leg. And that I could probably deal with. In his own way, he was kind of weirdly attractive.

"Never b'n with a girl," he said. "Not even girly-boys. Not sure's I want to, but mebbe I should. I could find out what I'm missin'." He shrugged. "Some o' the newcomers, they tell stories. I heard it both ways. Hard not to be curious. Some say it's better, some say it isn't, some say it's just a different kind of other. I think mebbe it tells more 'bout the teller than the tale, though." He stopped. "Y'r not sayin' much."

"Yeh. I'm not." I was listening to the way he spoke. His accent. His words. The rhythm of his phrasing. I would need to match it.

Something at the front of the vehicle beeped for attention then. He grabbed a handle and levered himself to his feet, clumping forward to the information bay. I wrapped the blanket around me and followed. He didn't stop me.

The vehicle slowed to a stop. The forward view was augmented, revealing the edge of a chasm. Overlays showed it to be Grand Canyon size. But deeper and wider.

"Nice view."

"Eastern edge," Mac said. "We turn south here." He tapped at his keyboard.

"What's all the hardware for?"

He swiveled to face me. "See, that's the real question I gotta answer? Were y' dropped out here to spy on us? I'd be real suspicious if y' was a biggun. But y'r not. So I don't have to be suspicious.

That's what makes me suspicious." He frowned. "Why are y' smilin'?"

"You think like me."

"Y' don' trust me neither?"

"Nope."

"Well, then—I guess we're even." He tapped at the controls in front of him, touching first one screen, then another. "There—" he pointed.

In front of us, the view cleared to show bright spotlit ovals tracing the ground. "See those —?"

Footprints. Huge footprints. Round and flat. A lot of them. Of course. Lower gravity, bigger animals.

"Big herd came down this way," Mac explained. "Every year, we track the migration. We tag the critters when we can. Sometimes somethin' panics 'em and a calf goes over the edge. Sometimes a mom. It happens. That's not the problem. The carrion-eaters—they're the problem. Especially the ones that fly. We don' like 'em gettin' too close."

He pointed toward another part of the display. "We're trackin' 'em. We got aerials watchin' them all the way south. And if we need, we can use the trucks to herd them away from places we don' want them stampin' through."

"That's a lot of firepower for a bunch of...

whatevers."

"It's not for the whatevers. We just use 'em for practice." Off my look, he said. "Nah, we don' shoot 'em. We just track 'em. I don' think they're very good eatin'. Some o' the boys mebbe. Not me."

"So, what's all the firepower for?"

Mac studied me for a moment. "Either y' know that or y' don't. If y' do know, then y'r askin' to make me think y' don't. And if y' don't know, then it's a fair question. So I still gotta wonder why y'r askin'."

"Because I'm curious?"

"Y' talk funny." He rubbed his nose, scratched his chin, considered the problem of me. "But I gotta think, ain't nobody comin' all the way out here on a one-way ticket just to spy on anythin' here. There's already enough empty pockets and loose mouths. Y' could buy 'em for cheap. Sendin' someone else don' make sense." He frowned. "Unless y'r here to sabotage somethin'." He squinted at me. "Are y'?"

"I'm just wondering how to get back home. I know you said it's impossible, but I hear the word impossible as a dare."

"Yah," he said. "Lotta guys talk like that. For the first few years anyway." He turned back to his controls and tapped a screen. The vehicle turned sharply, away from the chasm, and began rolling south.

Mac turned to face me. "Here's what y' gotta know. There's a lotta good people here. And a lotta not-so-good too."

He turned back to his controls, still explaining. "The original plan was t' create a monoculture. Y' know what that is, right? And it mostly worked. Still works. We mostly get guys who're okay with that. Some guys rechannel. Some guys are already that way. We get a trainload o' immigrants every month. Not all of 'em adjust well. But there's no goin' back. So, we kinda have t' work aroun' that. Nobody likes forced rechannelin', but—this ain't no libatarian annarky. If y' eat at our table, y' gotta do y'r share o' the work."

He brightened then, looked over at me. "But aside from that, it's mostly good. We been grown' our own babies for six generations now. We got a bunch o' tank-farms and we grow the kids already mono. If we're missin' anythin' not havin' women, most of us don' know it. We're gonna be fine. We got teachers sayin' that one day, most of us won't even know there's women. They'll just be some kind o' mythical creatures. Like rhinos and dodos. I dunno if that's true. Some o' the immigrants tell some pretty weird stories. And a lotta guys like to repeat 'em. I heard o' one fella—"

He stopped himself. "Y' ain't sayin' much."

"I won't be your slave," I said. "I won't be anybody's slave."

He reached forward and yanked a big red lever. The vehicle shuddered to a stop. "Y' want t' get out here?"

Shook my head. "No. I don't. I do appreciate your hospitality, Mac. You're a good guy. You probably saved my life. I owe you big time. And I will pay you back. I'll even work for you, if that's my best option. But I won't be your slave. I'm a free person. I won't indenture."

He frowned. He pursed his lips. His eyes narrowed. He studied me for a long moment —measuring, considering, turning thoughts over and looking to see what kind of bugs lurked underneath. Finally, he nodded. "'kay. I can go with that." He pushed the big red lever forward. The vehicle resumed its slow trundle across the terrain.

"So..." I said slowly. "If all this hardware isn't for killing big lumbering herds of whatevers, then what is it for?"

"It's for the war," he said.

"Oh," I said. "A war. Yeah. Good place for it. Out of the way."

"Yep," he agreed.

I played that back in my head. I was starting to sound stupid. I needed a rest.

But I had to know. "Who are you at war with?"

"Nobody. We're a test-bed. The company ships 'em out from Earth, we bash 'em around, find out how well they work. The other continent, that's the primary. Over here, we just play with the toys."

"Oh," I said. I'd have to ask about the details later. It was late, I'd gone too many hours without sleep. I was feeling my own exhaustion.

Mac noticed my yawn. He nodded toward the rear of the vehicle. "Y' wanna sleep, y' can bunk in the back. Still got some long hours t' go. There's sandwiches in the coldbox too."

With the blanket around me, I was getting close to warm again. It was scratchy, but I'd tuned out the worst of it. And I was honestly tired. I climbed into the back, found a bunk, and stretched out. It was almost comfortable. This truck or bus, whatever it was, it felt familiar. The way the bulkheads curved—

It took me a moment, then I realized. It was a capsule from the super-train—repurposed. Big enough to be a truck, a house, or a storage tank. Whatever you needed, the pods were fabbed for adaptive reuse, an additional resource for the onsite recipient. It was part of the shipping cost. Cheaper to fab a new one than pay for the cost of returning the empty.

That was interesting. It suggested that the super-trains had a direct route, through all the many portals and stations between here and Earth —possibly even a direct track all the way home. And that suggested the possibility of two-way traffic. That was *very* interesting. Another piece of the puzzle.

I fell asleep thinking about large trains pushing their way through holes in the space-time continuum. A lot of holes.

—and woke up almost immediately to someone crawling onto the bunk beside me, behind me, wrapping his arm around me and pulling me close against him, into a protecting embrace. He smelled good, he felt good, and I was really tempted. He was such a big, goofy, good-natured hunk of meat.

So tempted. But I was halfway between boy and girl. I'd been squeezing the noodle back out until he'd identified me as female. Not knowing what I should do, which way to go, I stopped. Now I was somewhere in the middle. Should I back up or go forward? There's a song we used to share, back in training, about being stuck in the middle of a shift.

If he was used to boys, if he preferred boys, I didn't have much to offer—and if he wanted a girl, well, I wasn't going to be able to accommodate him yet. And I don't roll over on my back on the first date anyway. Not even for flowers and chocolates. I'm not that kind of boy. Or girl. Although I do like chocolate. I wondered briefly if they had chocolate on this planet. They'd better—or that'd be another reason for not staying.

"Mmm," he said, nuzzling the back of my neck. He was gentle. That was a good beginning. And I did know a few ways to make a man happy that wouldn't make demands on my unfinished plumbing. But, no.

"Not now, please. It's too soon."

And that's when he made his mistake. "Hey —" He said. "All I done. Y' owe me—" He said it in a hurt tone, somewhere between pleading and demanding. That made it even more offensive.

I was tired, I was aching, I was sore all over, and I was stuck in the middle of a churning hormonal storm. I didn't know what sex I was right now or what I intended to be. Or maybe it was another lingering after-effect of the drugs. That might explain it, but it doesn't justify it. I reacted emotionally.

I yanked away from him, harder than I intended, whirled and kicked him in the stomach, right off the bunk. He went backward, slamming against the opposite bunk, and thudding to the floor awkwardly on his side—the plastic holster for his pistol snapped with a loud crack, which meant that he'd fallen square on it, which meant he'd fallen on his hip. That was going to hurt.

He came up red in the face, shock giving way to rage—

In another time and place, I would have killed him, could have killed him—

But I was physically drained. The broth he'd given me had contained an interesting mix of sedatives. Not enough to put me out, but enough to neutralize my ability to be a real threat. I realized that almost immediately after I'd kicked him. I was abruptly exhausted, too weak to move. Right. An adrenaline-triggered enervation. My heart pounded rapidly, trying to catch up.

That was all I had time to notice before he started beating me.

He was brutal. He was methodical. He used a closed fist. He yanked the blanket away. He punched my gut—hard! He punched the breath out of me. He punched me in the face. Repeatedly. I felt my nose crack. Possibly a cheekbone. He kneed me in the groin. Again and again. He said a bunch of words I didn't understand. Then he flung me face down on the bunk—

I passed out, but not before he finished. And not before I'd made up my mind to kill him. And I knew exactly how I was going to do it.

If I survived.

I ended up in a cage.

Mac had a couple of spare trucks following the one he was riding in. One of them was for holding runaway slaves. Yeah. That was his *other* business. Or hobby.

I should have figured that one out too.

I'd made too many mistakes. This was not the worst ever, but it was pretty bad. I was furious with myself.

This truck was another reconfigured cargo pod, spare and utilitarian. There was a control deck at the forward end, but it was powered down. Even if I could get out of the cage, I still didn't have the necessary passcodes.

It wasn't the worst possible cage. The floor was padded with memory-foam. I could sleep comfortably. There was a sanitation hole in the corner next to the wall. But there was no water spigot.

There were three other captives in the truck, each of us in our own narrow cage, barely enough room to lie down. Two of the men were Asian and didn't speak Spanglish or any other language I knew. The third was a tall thin black man with an accent thicker than he was, but I couldn't identify which part of the African continent he was from. He spoke to me in a broken dialect of Anglish, so I assumed somewhere up on the northeastern coast. But his voice had a soft lyrical lilt as well. Maybe he'd come from one of the breakaways in the Central Americas. His skin glittered with shiny dark scales and decorative patterns. I couldn't tell if they were genetic mods or after-market.

"Hey, you? Wakey-wake?"

I managed a weak nod.

"You a pretty one," he said. "Mac done you good, eh?"

I was too sore to speak, I managed a grunt.

He glanced up at the racks above us. "Long time till brekky. You need water, pretty boy. You don' look pink." He slid a transparent plastic bag through the bars. "It be slippy, but you need hydro more."

He was interrupted then. The two Asians began chattering at me, waving their arms, banging on the bars, trying to tell me something. It sounded like Chinese, but I didn't recognize any words. Not any language I knew.

The black man turned to them and said something in their own language. They shut up immediately.

"Dey say same thing. Water be slippy." He wiggled his fingers, then tapped his temple. "Take away anger-fight. I tell them I tell you. Drink now you." He pushed the water closer.

I took it gratefully. It had the same under taste as the broth. I could recognize it now. Nice to know. Not that I had a choice at the moment. I drank only a small amount, then started to pass it back.

The black man waved it off. "No. You keep. You need more. Me, I be part camel. On mother's side. Me father one horny bastid, y'know?" He smiled broadly, revealing sharpened teeth. A startling effect if you're not prepared for it, frightening in its implications.

He saw my expression. "No worry. I not be eating you." He laughed. "You too skinny." Then he added, "Besides, I be mostly farmer. Meat be expensive. And cruel. But fish…?" He rubbed his stomach. "Fish be good. Many good fish this world. Nobody hungry" He pointed to his sharpened teeth. "No worry. These be for war. Bite badman, he die. Long time, much pain. Even if he live, still long time, much pain. So you be askin' now, how did stupid me end up in cage like pretty you?"

He thumped his chest, "I be Talla-Talla Manfella. I come this world many long times ago, with fathers and brothers. I be so small, I ride in pocket. Family come out here to farback, long way from nastymans. Hard struggle long time, two brothers die. But we make it. Den nastymans come with trucks. Machines. Big lights. Make—" He frowned, momentarily frustrated. "—sorry, I not have all words. Make big noises. Boom! Boom! Everywhere. Many die. I lose one father, two more brothers. All de rest taken in trucks. Never see again. I hide. Dey never find me. Many times dey come, dey look. Dey never find me." Then he added sadly, "Until now. Catch me with lights." He pointed at the roof, at the sky on the other side of it. "Cannot hide from lights that follow. Night-breakers. Dey drop nets from sky. I be dead soon.

You will sing for me? Sing me over?"

"Sing you over—?"

He fumbled for the words. "Sing me across? To de sky?"

"I—I don't know. I mean, I don't know how, "I admitted. "I've never had to—"

"Is not hard. Sing from de heart, yes?"

"But we just met, I don't know you—"

"I give you water. That be enough. You give me song, yes?"

Such a simple request. But I still hesitated—

Talla-Talla put his hands on the bars between us and stared at me intensely. "I not have anyman for word-speak. Not for many long times. Do it right, yes?"

"Do it very right, yes," I said, my voice cracking. "Very good."

"You have name?" he asked earnestly.

"Yes." I tapped my own chest. "I be—in my words, I am Slither."

"Slither? Like snake?"

I nodded.

"Good name. I like. You slither out of here soon, you get away. I die. You sing."

I didn't see how that was a good bargain, but I nodded. I liked the part about me getting away.

68

Over the next few days, Talla-Talla-Manfella and I had a lot of time to talk. He and his family hadn't come from Earth at all. They were five generations removed. They'd lived three stations down the line, on a world that was mostly islands and had been settled by Somalis, Nigerians, Jamaicans, and various other political refugees who thought to create a new black homeland. They'd left when religious and tribal fanatics had clashed. The islands were apparently not big enough for all.

This world, Sparta, was a whole other story. Too much land, not enough people. Most of the official settlements were on the other continent, connected by doglegs of land that served as sometime bridges, depending on the weather, but one could also sail across any of several narrow straits that were open all year long.

Consequently, there were a lot of unlicensed settlements on this side of the planet—and a lot of places where escaped slaves hid out too. So it was all fair game for slavers and bounty-hunters. When Mac and his Pa weren't playing war games and weren't tracking whatevers, they hunted for other opportunities.

The auto-kitchen dropped a ration-pack into the cages every six hours. The water had the same funny taste, more of the drug, but I had to stay hydrated. I didn't have a choice. As long as I didn't excite myself, I might be okay. If I had time, I could finish my shift to male. Well, just the plumbing. That I could do. And Mac would look like an idiot if he tried to sell me as the only female on a male planet.

The real problem was I didn't have the resources for shifting. I'd exhausted my fat stores and the ration-packs falling out of the auto-kitchen were the wrong side of spare.

Without protein, I couldn't bulk up my muscles. Without fat, I wouldn't have the energy for the process. Without water—well, without water, I couldn't do anything. Even bad water. I can filter a lot of crap, but I still need something to start with.

The next time I woke up, there were three ration packs and two water-bubbles pushed into my cage.

"What's this?"

Talla-Talla turned around to look at me. He stretched as best he could. I could hear the bones in his neck cracking as he bent his head from side to side. "You be gettin' strong now, yes."

"But this is yours. And theirs—" I pointed to the two Chinese.

"I be camel," Talla-Talla said. "Dey be deadmen."

"I don't understand."

"Nuttin' to unnerstan'. Dey be dyin'. Not be

slaves never. Die instead. Hope to die before we get dere. Mebbe they will, mebbe they won't. Dey give you this, yes?"

"I can't take it. I can't."

"Go to waste then. Better it go to waist." He patted his belly.

I shook my head and backed away. Something about this was very wrong. But my head was too fuzzy to sort it all out. And I was hungry. Very hungry. And thirsty. I needed the protein and carbohydrates and fat. And especially the water.

I curled up facing the wall, clutching my growling belly, trying to convince myself to be selfish. I could use those resources. If they weren't going to—

But I didn't have the right to—

Or did I—?

Did the two Chinese care if I ate their rations? If they were determined to die, and if it would help me survive, then shouldn't I? Especially if it would help me escape. And maybe I could help them escape? No, that was a fantasy. Whatever I chose here—

Mom's words came back to me then. "Always take care of your own well-being first. Otherwise, you have nothing to give to anyone else."

Yes, it would be selfish to eat those rations.

But it would be the right kind of selfishness. Oh, hell—

I rolled away from the wall and grabbed the packs. Talla-Talla had been watching me the whole time. He smiled and nodded. I didn't like that. I knew he meant well, but for someone who'd been living on his own for as long as he said, why was he so gregarious? Why was he being so friendly to me? Was he that desperate for a friend?

I ate slowly. Thinking.

I wouldn't have enough protein to start bulking up my muscles, but I could start the process of stretching my bones and expanding my rib cage. I wasn't going to worry about healing the damage from Mac's beating. I didn't know how long it would take to get to the slave market, but I had no intention of looking good for any prospective buyer. I left my nose to heal at a terrible angle and I didn't regrow any of the missing teeth. I thought about letting one eye go lame and discolored, but held back on that— it was still swollen shut. I did spend some time remodeling my ears to stick out in an unbalanced and misshapen way. I let large patches of my hair fall out too.

I hadn't done hideous in a while, I was out of practice and I probably overdid it, but the more I thought about it, the more I wanted Mac to think he'd beaten me ugly and significantly lowered my market value. If I'd had more time, I would have twisted one shoulder down and grown a hump on the other. I had a feeling I was going to be on this planet longer than I wanted.

But I had to be careful. I didn't want Talla-Talla to recognize that I was shifting. I had to make it look like I was healing—that most of the ugly was really me underneath the beating.

After four uninterrupted days, the truck stopped—

Sparta days—36 metric hours. 144 total.

Talla-Talla shared what his fathers and brothers had taught him. Sparta is near the outer edge of the Goldilocks zone, most of the time anyway, but its orbit is just elliptical enough and off-center enough that sometimes it flirts dangerously with the inner and outer edges of the zone. It makes for some interesting seasons, at least eight in any given year, sometimes more.

During inner-summer, noontime temperatures in the so-called "temperate zone" usually hover between 50 and 60 Celsius, then because of the lower-than-Earth air pressure at what passes for sea level, nighttime in the desert usually drops to freezing. Or below. Outer-winter produces CO_2 frost in the polar regions.

Considering all the possibilities, I was lucky, I'd been dropped in the temperate zone, shortly after sunset, when most of the day's heat was still seeping out of the land. Or had that timing been intentional? Maybe I was supposed to be discovered. Well, slaves are valuable, yes. Somebody must have known where Mac was patrolling. They might even have alerted him. "Hey, we're dropping off a little package for you."

So maybe it was all planned out. Maybe this stop as well. The truck shuddered to a halt without warning. Everything but the air conditioning shut down. Only a few standby lights stayed on.

There were no windows, so as near as I could tell, we could have been parked on a busy city street or sitting in the middle of nowhere. I guessed the middle of nowhere. Something was going on somewhere. Whatever it was, we weren't invited. So that suggested it was bad news either way.

If Mac and company lost, then we would be stuck here, caged and abandoned. If Mac and company won, our situation wasn't going to get any better. Either way, it was out of our control. Talla-Talla was strangely silent, as if listening through the walls. When I asked him what was happening, he just shook his head sadly. "It be bad, whatever."

SEVEN

We were awakened by the truck doors clacking open. Actinic blue light roared sideways through the door, outlining everything with harsh brown shadows—so bright I had to cover my eyes with my forearm. Blinking against the glare, I saw three gaunt figures stumble into the truck. The pod groaned and leaned under the sudden weight—behind them, Mac, wearing helmet and goggles and armor, waving that same huge rifle he'd pointed at me the night we met.

He directed the new captives into three separate cages. One beside me, on the side away from Talla-Talla, two opposite. Those two looked as if they'd been beaten. The one in the cage next door was a boy, not much bigger than me. They wore simple, rough-hewn garments—shapeless bags mostly, like burlap or canvas. Escapees? Rags around their feet instead of shoes. But it was more than I had. I still had only a blanket.

Mac barely glanced at me. He didn't speak to anyone else either. He looked like his face hurt from the inside. Bitter, mean, ugly, unhappy. Not too hard to understand. You didn't become a slaver if your heart was full of love for your fellow man.

As soon as the cages were locked and secured, Mac exited. After a bit more, something underneath the floor whined back to life and the truck resumed its slow steady trundle across the unseen desert.

One of the men opposite began weeping softly. The other made an effort to comfort him through the bars. Both spoke in a language I didn't understand. The boy in the cage next to me looked around curiously, studied me for a moment, but didn't speak. I think we were all afraid of each other. What if one of us was really a spy? Not that there was anything to discover by spying. But... I knew of situations where loose remarks behind bars exposed some very dark secrets. Worse than murder.

I rolled myself back up in my blanket and faced the wall.

During training, we'd been beaten, bashed, and brutalized. We'd been exposed to as many different forms of emotional and physical torture as our trainers could imagine, the most extreme endurance tests possible.

As we approached the end of the training, after we had lost all those who weren't going to make it, after the rest of us were no longer crying ourselves to sleep or cursing our trainers, after we had gotten over the emotional hump and it was clear that we were beginning to own our new abilities—during one of the classroom discussions, "context-setting" they called it, one of the coaches acknowledged what we had already figured out.

"Yes," she said. "Our intention is to be rougher on you than anything you might ever experience out there in the field. Whatever gets thrown at you out there, we want you to say, 'I can' handle this. I've been through worse.'"

And for the most part, she was right.

This situation was the exception.

Always before, I could see an endgame and more than a few ways to get there. I could point myself down the path of success, or failing that, the path of escape. But neither of those avenues existed here, not even a foot trail.

I was going to need one hell of an opportunity—what we in the biz call "a snowball on the day-side of Mercury"—if I was going to effect even the smallest change in my circumstances. The one thing that had been repeatedly beaten into all of us was that there are no such things as fortunate coincidences, and don't even use the word "miracle." You survive by distrusting every opportunity. Other people can have accidents, you can't.

But...assuming that the other prisoners

really were prisoners, and I couldn't see any reason to doubt that, then if I could get them talking, I might learn a little more about this place called Sparta.

It was a place to start.

The boy in the cage next to me was barely into his teens. Still had a bit of baby fat. His hands were as soft as his features. He wasn't a field hand and he likely wasn't going to be sold as a laborer. I wondered what his backstory was. How did he get here? And why was he wearing an old canvas dress?—no, just some kind of a bag with holes cut into it for head and arms—the same as the two he'd been brought in with. Their other clothes had been taken away. Probably some very nice clothes, worth stealing. And that suggested that whatever other supplies and tools they might have had, had also been confiscated. Stolen. A vehicle perhaps? A burrow or a pod? Maybe someone had sold them some goods with tracking devices embedded and that's how they'd been caught...?

But the boy didn't speak any language I understood, so I couldn't ask him. And I wasn't sure I wanted Talla-Talla interpreting for me. If he really was what he said he was, then he shouldn't have all the knowledge he claimed to have.

So I meditated and concentrated on building up my muscles. While the others slept, I stretched and exercised beneath my blanket. I had no idea what any of the others might have thought about the slow bumping and moaning and gasping. None of them would meet my gaze anymore and I had a feeling Talla-Talla had told them some bizarre story about me. Either that or the ugly was working.

Four more impossible days and two more captures. Mac was having a good roundup. And I was getting stronger. I was careful not to let it show. I still hunched small and ugly.

Talla-Talla kept passing me ration-packs from the Chinese, they were both getting very weak by now. They lay on the floor of their separate cages and barely moved. The newcomers kept their rations and kept to themselves. They did look at me curiously when Talla-Talla passed me the extras. I guess they thought I was his kept boy.

Talla-Talla had appointed himself the king of the truck, but because we were all locked in separate cages, there wasn't much he could do but talk. If I didn't want to talk to him, I pretended to sleep. He wondered aloud why I wasn't getting fat. I wasn't going to tell him I was reconstructing myself, but I ate everything he gave me and drank the water too. Some of it I used for washing, but not much. And what passed for a toilet wasn't much more than a hole with a snap-seal cover. I supposed the waste went into a tank where it was processed for methane and fertilizer.

By the time we picked up the last two captives—Mac had bought them from another trucker, I wasn't talking to anyone, not even Talla-Talla much. I pretended to be sick and I coughed a lot. It wasn't all performance. Shifting is painful.

I tried to do most of the work while the others were sleeping, but my occasional gasps of pain—and once even a scream—sometimes woke one or another. The scream woke all of them and they gave me curious stares, but I just rolled over and faced the wall and didn't bother to control my trembling. I needed them to think I was suffering from some condition they couldn't define. I wanted Mac to think I was dying.

My body didn't look any bigger, but inside... well, the first time I could get a good grip on Mac's throat—or any other suitably tender part of his anatomy, I had a particular part in mind—I intended to detach it rapidly and painfully.

After another interminable period of traveling, the ride became turbulent, with the truck bouncing and rocking sideways.

"Big wind," said Talla-Talla. "Grandfather storm."

The wind kept slamming us sideways. And then we heard a steady pattering on the roof and one wall. Sleet and hail. The noise grew louder and more intense, a jack-hammering racket. The hail stones must have been the size of golf balls.

"No be lookin' a-me. I never come dis far south."

"How do you know we're heading south?"

"Grandfather storm live by de scorch-belt, pretty one."

"Scorch-belt?"

"De belt around de planet waist. Always big-hot."

"So why are we going there?"

"Oh, we not go all de way. We just go alla stormland."

"What's at stormland?"

"De train. I tink."

"You don't know?"

"I never see myself. I only know from travelers. Dey tell me. Dis where train leaves for other side. De other land."

"The other continent?"

"Continnit?" He struggled with the word, gave up. "If you say other land, yes." He looked sad then. "We be gone slave market. Biggest of all probly."

The wall of the truck *whomped* as a sudden burst of wind slammed sideways into us. It pushed us so hard it felt we were toppling. Then the autopilot corrected and started turning into the wind. The vehicle righted itself with another bang.

"Dat not be good," said Talla-Talla. He looked ashen.

I didn't answer. I was wondering if the next big gust would roll us over and if so, would it crack the pod wide open? And if it did, would I be safer staying inside? Or should I risk exposure to the storm? What if the wind was strong enough to roll the pod across the terrain like a tumbleweed? If I held onto the bars of the cage, anchoring myself, it'd be a wild ride, but survivable. Outside of the truck, maybe not so.

Considered it. Yeah. No. I'd be better off if the truck stayed shiny-side-up.

Another gust of wind, this one worse than the last, but the truck finished turning into it and even though we rocked violently for a minute or three, we stayed vertical. The hammering on the roof and sides continued. The pod itself creaked and groaned. The wind was growling now, a strange deep rumble that seemed to shake the whole world.

Then the storm got stronger and the truck had to tack its way through the gusts, angling back and forth like a sailboat fighting an uncooperative wind. I didn't know if I should be anxious or grateful that the truck didn't have windows and the displays were off. I decided to be anxious. I'd rather see the monster under the bed than have to imagine it.

We bumped and banged our way through the storm for what must have been hours. We had no way to tell. Not being able to tell made me wish I'd gone in for some of the more sophisticated implants—except even the simplest scan can revealed non-biological implants and there are times when a shifter doesn't want those kinds of questions raised.

And then abruptly, the ride smoothed out. We were rolling on a paved surface. The wind still rocked the truck, the hail still pounded, but it seemed obvious that we were approaching the local equivalent of civilization—civilized enough for paved roads anyway.

Another little bit and we were rolling upward, possibly a 5% grade. The buffeting of the wind and the hammering of the hail stopped as completely as if a switch had been thrown. We had to be inside a tunnel.

Then the wind and hail hit us again— we were out of the tunnel. The truck turned and angled left. We began descending, possibly spiraling down the inside of a crater. If there was a lake at the bottom, then the side of the crater would be a very convenient site for a station.

We rolled for a while, and then for a while longer, and finally the truck lurched to a halt. We still had some wind, not as much as before. Only the barest hint of rain remained. We'd gone through a tunnel, so I assumed we were somewhere on the leeward side of the ridge, probably a few miles around and down. Big crater.

I looked to see how the others were doing. If the Chinese weren't dead, they were close to it. I couldn't see if they were breathing. In the cell next to me, the soft boy began crying in helpless terror. Talla-Talla was still sleeping. That was weird, but no weirder than anything else he'd said or done.

Nothing happened for a long time. We waited, then we waited some more. The auto-kitchen dropped ration-packs. After we ate, we waited again. I napped for a while, considered my options—I didn't have any—rolled over and went back to sleep. Another set of ration-packs dropped. And then a lot more nothing happened.

And then, finally, in the middle of more nothing happening, the door to the truck clacked open and harsh blue light dazzled and glared and outlined everything and we all had to shield our eyes. Two bulky figures in armor and faceless helmets climbed in. They carried serious-looking stun-guns. The pod creaked and sagged under their weight. Wordlessly, they began unlocking cages and waving us out.

I grabbed my blanket, wrapping it tight around myself, but one of them yanked it away and tossed it aside, leaving me naked and gasping as I stepped out into the cold night air. No ladder down. A concrete platform right up to the hatch— bright lights blazed overhead. Bitter winds swept sideways. Icy needles caught me in the eyes. As fast as I shook the rain away, new spatters stung me.

Almost immediately I was shivering, not totally a performance. I hadn't had time to self-insulate.

There were more guards strung out in a line. We were on a concrete deck under a high canopy. Whatever else there was, I couldn't tell. It was impossible to see anything beyond the painful lights.

The subzero torrents made it difficult, almost impossible, to self-regulate my body temperature. I hugged myself and danced up and down, trying to keep warm. Someone poked me with the cold barrel of a rifle. I jumped away, hurried to follow the soft boy. He was still crying, wiping his eyes and his nose with the back of his hands. The two most recent captives were ahead of him. Behind me were the two who'd been caught with the boy. Talla-Talla was last in line. I tried looking back to see if anyone was retrieving the dead Chinese, but the guard poked me forward again.

With the ice blowing into my eyes, I couldn't see where we were going. On one side of us, there was the line of guards. On the other side, nothing—just a black emptiness that suggested a bigger emptiness beyond. Blasts of wind came howling out of it, driving stinging flurries of ice and snow. There was no railing at the edge of the concrete, nor guards, which suggested a pretty good incentive not to go there. The wind screamed up from a long ugly drop. The blue fingers of the spotlights occasionally poked into that gloom. If there was a bottom, I couldn't see it. Maybe they intended it as an option.

They lined us up facing the wall of darkness and the blinding wind, with guards in front of us and behind us. A fat man, not a guard but obviously in charge, walked the length of the line, squinting at each of us in turn. He carried a baton and occasionally poked at one or another of the prisoners. His face was florid and he wore a heavy fur-lined coat, floor-length. Mac followed him, halfway between puffed up and deferential. Mac hugged layers of blankets around himself. The guards wore heavy longshirts, almost to their ankles.

None of the prisoners were dressed for the cold. Those of us who weren't naked wrapped their arms around themselves and shivered. If this went on much longer, we were all going to get frostbite. Not a good way to treat the inventory, but the Fat Man either didn't care or he was oblivious to the wind.

When the fat man got to me, he paused. He turned to Mac and asked him something in an unrecognizable language. Mac answered in the same language. The fat man looked skeptical. He peered at me again. He poked at my groin with his baton, forcing my legs apart. He bent to look at my genitals. There wasn't much, just a nub, but it was convincing enough.

The fat man straightened and snarled something at Mac. Mac nodded his head and insisted. The fat man shook his head and insisted louder. I heard the word "shifter" and I kept myself from smiling. The fat man didn't believe Mac's story. I was a skinny little boy, naked and half-starved—and neither Mac nor the fat man had the equipment to scan me and discover otherwise.

Mac kept arguing, Fat Man kept shaking his head. Finally, Fat Man said something loud and rude and turned away. I didn't have to understand his language to know what he said to Mac. "You're an idiot. Don't you know a penis when you see one?" He moved on, grumbling. Mac glared at me. I studied the ground between us and kept my face impassive.

Now Fat Man moved to face the crying boy. The boy sniffled and tried to look brave, even meeting Fat Man's evaluating gaze. Fat Man poked the boy with his baton, held it up to his cheek, forcing him to turn his head this way and that. He held up a hand and snapped his fingers, one of the guards stepped forward. Fat Man snapped an order. The guard unsheathed a knife and sliced open the oversized bag the boy wore as a dress. It fell around his feet. The boy's skin reddened immediately, scoured by the gritty blasts of wind and ice.

Another snapped command and the guard quickly turned the boy around so Fat Man could look at his backside. The guard bent the boy over, then spread his butt cheeks to reveal the secret rosebud. Fat Man grunted, satisfied, and the guard straightened the boy and faced him around again. Fat Man nodded, even allowed himself a smile. He pulled off a glove and stroked the boy, starting with his cheek, down the side of his neck, across a nipple, down his soft belly, and then to—

That's when the boy screamed, more words I couldn't understand. Breaking free, he threw himself sideways, catching the guards by surprise. There was nowhere to go, but he already knew that. He dodged sideways around the fat man, leapt forward and hurled himself over the edge and into the darkness below. The wind caught him for half a second, then he was gone.

He disappeared so quickly into the darkness it seemed like a mistake, a hallucination of the storm—one of the spotlights swung over curiously, revealing nothing but the depth of the gloom below.

The two men who'd been captured with him screamed in horrified anguish—but their guards quickly blocked them following.

And then, we were all frozen in place. Nobody moving. Not the prisoners, not the guards. Everyone waited for some sign from the Fat Man.

The Fat Man seemed to harden where he stood. His expression tightened. He rubbed his forehead, thinking. Then he made a decision. He shouted something hard at the closest guards, then pointed to Mac. They hesitated, then grinned. Mac raised his hands, shouting what must have been words for, "No, not me! No!"

But the guards ignored him. They grabbed him, pulled his heavy blankets away, cut his clothes off him, stripped him naked in seconds, everything but his boots, and pushed him into the line where the crying boy had been, Mac still screaming his outrage and his innocence.

Fat Man shouted another order and waved at the prisoners to move out. The guards began poking us with their rifles, shouting and shoving us roughly. As if on cue, the ice storm picked up again, sending sheets of bitterness sideways across the slippery deck. I was beyond cold, beyond shivering, amazed I hadn't already passed out.

Ahead, darkness pierced by a hole of light, maybe a door. If it got me out of the cold, that would be fine. I hurried after Mac—and then I was through the hole in the wall and into the light where another guard pushed me into another cage. This pod was exactly like the one we'd left. No windows, cages on both sides. The only difference, I had no blanket here. I thought about saying something but decided not to bother. I sat down in my cage, wrapped my arms around my knees, went into a meditative state and methodically began lowering my body temperature. I could survive

20 Celsius by going into near-hibernation, but it wouldn't be comfortable. I decided to drop far enough to stop wasting energy trying to maintain normal body heat. Room temp would do it.

Mac was shoved into a cage of his own, not so confident anymore. He looked stricken. Understandable—he knew how slaves were treated on this world. To his credit, he would be the most dangerous kind of slave—the kind who knew the weaknesses of the slaveholders. He stood up in his cage and began screaming protests. If anyone heard him, they paid no attention.

The door to the pod was still open. Talla-Talla hadn't been pushed in yet. I could hear some kind of discussion just beyond the door. Talla-Talla was talking to someone in that same unrecognizable language. It sounded like they were questioning him.

Then there was silence. Just a heartbeat—followed by the sound of someone being struck several times—and then Talla-Talla Manfella was thrown roughly into the pod. He landed hard on the floor, leaving a crimson streak where he fell. His nose and mouth were bleeding profusely. One guard pushed him into the cage across from me, the other kicked it shut.

Mac started shouting even louder now, even more intensely. He babbled furiously at the guard. Whatever the guards' reaction, their expressions were hidden behind the black faceplates of their helmets. If they were communicating with each other, we couldn't hear, but abruptly one approached Mac cautiously.

Maybe the guard was sympathetic. His body language shifted. He seemed to be listening to Mac's unending stream of invective and promises. Apparently convinced, the guard now detached something from his chest-plate, reached through the bars and held it against Mac's chest—right above the sternum. Mac had just enough time to shriek, "Nooo—" Then something buzzed and he collapsed to the floor, the device still attached to his body. A flat black disk.

The guards left, closing the hatch behind them. We could have been in the same truck we'd just left, except this wasn't a truck. We were aboard a train made of the same kind of cargo pods. Just before being pushed in, I'd glimpsed a long line of pods stretching ahead into the gloom. If what Talla-Talla had told me was accurate, we were on our way to the other continent—where the portal was.

That was good news. Maybe. Okay, useful. I'd be closer to home. Well, the chance to get home— if I could figure out how to get through however many layers of quarantine between here and there. But at least I was headed in the right direction.

Nothing happened for the next couple of hours. We heard distant thumps and bumps as other pods were loaded. I ignored all of Talla-

Talla's attempts to start a conversation. I had to concentrate on saving my energy resources. Then the door clacked open and another dozen captives were pushed into cages, until every cage had two prisoners—except the one with Mac. He was still unconscious. Probably an induced meditative state, useful for transporting prisoners. Probably how I was transported here. That was another question. Did I have an unknown vulnerability? If that was the case, was there a protection? Something to investigate. In all my spare time.

After a short consultation—I assumed it was a consultation, two of the guards stood and looked at each other for a bit, they must have been talking on an internal comm channel—they pushed Talla-Talla in with me. I didn't know if that was a good sign or an ominous one. Or just coincidence.

Nope. It couldn't be a coincidence. I didn't believe in them. I put my head back down between my knees.

Almost immediately, Talla-Talla was grabbing me, shaking me.

"Pretty one! Wake up, you!"

I'd gotten my body temperature halfway down to room temperature. My skin must have looked blue, almost cyanotic—

"You not be dyin' on me now!" He kept shaking me, hard.

"I'm not dying! Stop it!"

"You damn-damn cold!" He opened his shirt and pulled me close against him, against his naked skin. He wrapped me tight inside his arms. I relaxed and leaned back against his bare skin. His scales were smoother all the way down from his chest to his belly—and hot to the touch. "You be too cold, too cold much-much. I fix. Me hotter than you, much-much. I be hot desert-boy, not you."

I shut up and let him hold me. His body temperature had to be four or five degrees higher than my normal. Or maybe he was designed to hold heat in against the night. Or maybe I was doing him a favor. All of life is about heat dissipation. That's one theory anyway.

Maybe Talla-Talla was semi-reptilian, able to regulate his body temp to match the conditions of his environment. It wasn't impossible. If his scales were thermal operators, he was probably better suited for it than I was.

I didn't question it. I just leaned back and enjoyed the warmth. This was the warmest I'd been since arriving on this planet. "Make you some warm skin soon, yes?"

I grunted something that could have been an agreement, then fell asleep in his arms. He woke me up when the auto-kitchen dropped ration-packs. These were fatter than the ones in Mac's truck. Talla-Talla only ate part of his and passed the rest to me. "You eat, I be fine." I didn't argue.

Eventually, after another hour of waiting, a guard entered carrying something that looked like a backpack. He entered Mac's cage and attached various tubes and hoses from the device to various parts of Mac's body—a tube down his throat, a face mask, a catheter, an anal catheter, and a few monitor chips here and there. Interesting. It suggested two things—one, they wanted to keep Mac in his induced meditation for a while, possibly as long as a week. And two, this was going to be a long journey.

I could understand why they hadn't put Mac in a cage with anyone else. If they'd put him in with me, I'd have likely killed him. And maybe eaten him as well. I'm not fussy. Protein is protein.

The guard left and a few minutes later, after a series of beeps and buzzes and other readiness noises, the train began easing forward. We were on our way, sliding toward tomorrow—not too fast at first. We angled around and upward. The rattle of hail resumed, along with the hard buffeting of the wind, though not as bad as when we were in a single truck—through a long tunnel, probably not the same one we'd come through before, and then we were accelerating down around the outer wall of the crater, almost gliding now.

This was familiar tech—a standard for all the portal trains, efficient lo-fab printing. The trains and trucks all used the same rubbery wheels

—semi-solid honeycombs that functioned both as wheels and shock absorbers. The treads were shaped to ride within the polycarbonized tracks. The tracks were prefab units, easily joined. So were the towers that held the sections twenty to thirty meters above the ground. This would keep the trains above the local wildlife, above floods, above (most) sand dunes, and above any hasty attempts to intercept them. You couldn't stop a train short of destroying the tracks. And if you did that, the built-in monitors would alert any oncoming trains and whatever authority was responsible for maintaining order.

The trains didn't run on top of the rails as much as they ran between them. The cargo sections filled the bottom half, along with the various life-support systems. The top half of the pods were living spaces or more cargo. Running the trains between the rails made for stability and reduced wind-buffeting. But we could still feel the relentless storm pounding and buffeting the carriage.

How did I know all this? Research. The portal economy depended on the railroads. Several hundred thousand kilometers of track connected all the different worlds through all the different portals—a vast web of interconnections. The rails were the bonds that tied the worlds together.

For most of the ride, Talla-Talla sat leaning against the wall with me held tightly in his lap, his shirt wrapped firmly around me. Not my preferred method of travel, but better than freezing. The only problem, I couldn't do much internal rebuilding, I didn't want him aware of the shifting within my body, so I stored everything in my second stomach, slowed my digestion down to idle, and wished for a blanket. Or clothes. Or even a hot fudge sundae.

I mean, as long as I was wishing....

EIGHT

T he first time I shifted, I wasn't yet four. We were at the beach. It was the first day of spring and the water was still very cold. The older children were so excited to finally get aboveground that they didn't care. They just pulled off all their clothes and charged into the water naked, laughing and screaming and yelling. So of course, all the younger children did the same. We struggled out of our shorts and longshirts and went running into the water too—and just as quickly came running out again, screaming how cold it was. We did that several times, each time trying to prove that we were just as brave as the big kids.

We finally did get used to the water enough to splash around in it, shrieking and splashing each other, running into the waves and running out again. I remember feeling a little uncomfortable, like I had to pee, but I didn't think anyone would mind if I peed in the ocean. But when I finally did come out, my older sister pointed and laughed. "Look, Bobba's ittle willy has fallen off. I bet a fish ate it." I looked down, she was right, my willy was gone. I screamed in anguish and ran for Manya. I didn't know that it had retracted in the cold water, and I didn't know that Dilla was joking. I didn't know about shifting and I didn't know about jokes. I thought a fish *had* bitten it off.

When Manya tells the story, she says I screamed for an hour, insisting that somebody should go back into the water and find it, before a fish really did eat it. Manya says I also begged Datya not to punish me for losing my willy: "It wasn't my fault. I didn't know it was loose. If we find it can we sew it back on? How am I going to pee?"

Finally, Datya wrapped me in a towel and carried me off to the bus to comfort me. I remember he held me and rocked me until I stopped crying. And then he explained that my willy hadn't fallen off, it had just pulled back inside for a while, because now it was time for me to be a girl. Like Dilla. I was mostly worried that it would never come back, I liked my willy and I wasn't sure that I wanted to be a girl, but Datya said that it was more fun to be a girl than a boy and he was looking forward to the time when he could become a woman again.

That was when I stopped crying. Datya, a woman? I couldn't imagine it and at first I thought he was telling me a make-believe. But he promised to show me pictures when we got home. "You don't remember that I carried you in my tummy, do you?

You'll see. We have pictures."

When we went back to the others, I ran up to Dilla and said, "It didn't fall off. You lied. I'm a girl now. Like you. So there."

The next time I shifted, I was five. I had fallen into the habit of rubbing myself through the soft cotton of my nightgown before falling asleep, and I noticed a hard bump. At first, I thought it was because of what I was doing—but then I remembered something in one of the bedtime books that Manya read to me. Manya was a man by then. So I got out of bed and padded down the hall and asked Manya to look. "Is my willy coming back? Am I going to be a boy now?" He didn't even need to look; he just hugged me and said, "You're right on schedule." That was all I needed to hear, I went back to bed. And in the next few days I found a whole different way to rub myself that was nice too.

I shifted again just before I turned seven. This time, I sort of expected it. For a few days before it started, I was having strange gooshy feelings. I went to Datya and told her that I felt like another change was coming on. Datya agreed and we went shopping for new clothes. I was a little embarrassed, looking at the skirts and panties and other things, but I wasn't the only boy there.

The shopkeeper was a young man wearing a denim skirt and a friendly smile. He saw me frowning skeptically at a display of frilly dresses and led me off to a rack of pleated kilts instead. "Here, these make a lot more sense. Don't ever buy anything you're not wildly excited about. Otherwise, it'll just get old in the closet. If you don't see anything you like on this rack, there are longshirts over here." And then he added, almost in a whisper so Datya couldn't hear. "Wear what makes you happy."

I was fingering a plaid wraparound, but it was heavier than I wanted. "It's okay," I said. "It's not my first time in a dress. I was a girl when I was little."

"That's good," he said. "But sometimes boys your age are a little shy about the change."

I shrugged, kind of admitting that he was right. "Yeah." I headed toward the longshirts. "Do you have anything in gray or blue? Something lightweight?"

I wore mostly longshirts for the next year or two, not just because they were comfortable, but because they were good for covering up my shyness.

I shifted back to male just before my ninth birthday, but I kept wearing longshirts because they were easy and comfortable. A couple months after that, Manya and Datya asked me if I wanted to go pro, like Dilla and Auncle Dri. I'd have to start soon if that was something I wanted to do. I said okay and went into training, four hours a day, nine on weekends.

Later on, full-time.

NINE

I lost track of time, passing in and out of consciousness. Mostly, it was deliberate. I let Talla-Talla think I was dying of exposure. In reality, I was conserving energy and focusing on muscle strength. With my eyes closed I stepped through the memories of my exercises and trainings. Not quite muscle-memory, but good enough to keep me focused.

Talla-Talla woke me whenever the ration-packs dropped, insisting that I eat and drink my fill. He didn't have to insist, I would have done it anyway, but I put on a convincing performance of being too weak and feeble to eat without help.

A couple of days into the trip, the train had stopped for a few hours, probably to load or unload supplies, maybe to take on a few more captives. But whoever was in charge finally revived Mac. He didn't speak to any of the rest of us, he stayed wrapped up in the corner of his cage. And the rest of us mostly kept our backs turned to him. He was not one of us. Then we were on our way again.

Internally, I was pretty sure we traveled at

least four days, maybe five. I could have been mistaken. Eventually, a shift in sound—and speed —suggested we were passing through a tunnel, a very long one, several hours long, probably passing beneath the scorch belt of the equator, and possibly on to the other continent.

I had no idea of the geography of this world. None of the other captives in the car had any but the vaguest idea. Even Talla-Talla's information was sketchy. Apparently, that information was restricted—most likely to limit a slave's ability to escape. A very old technique.

I was beginning to get it, slavery on this planet wasn't just an indenture. It was a long-term institution. And as long as the slaveholders had heavy-duty technology, a slave revolt was as unlikely as a chorus line of dancing unicorns singing the big hits of Igor Stravinsky in a sold-out concert at Shea Stadium—because Shea Stadium was no longer there.

At last, finally—at least a day after the tunnel, we were on an easy slope, descending for the better part of an hour, until at last we could feel the train coasting, slowing, and finally rolling the last few meters to a gentle stop.

Nothing happened for a while. That was to be expected. Whoever was running this show had made it clear that we were unimportant to the point of being disposable. We weren't the best cargo for slavers. We were a pretty shabby-looking lot. Living a hard-scrabble life, trying to scrape existence out of a naked landscape hardens you only if you survive. Maybe Mac might be worth something, he had a good build, he could probably work.

At last, the door popped open. Two guards came in. They opened Mac's cage and dragged him out by the arms. He didn't resist. I'd have expected him to protest, but I think his spirit was broken—he was that brittle. They pulled him out the door and they were gone. But they left the door open. Bright light streamed in. Faint sounds of people and machines. Unfamiliar smells—hints of sweat, cleansing fluids, and . . . I couldn't identify the rest. Maybe some kind of spice?

I considered my options. I'd already figured out how to escape from the cage, that would have been the easy part. But I had no idea what was outside that door. Without a map, without a plan, I wouldn't get very far.

A couple of young men, well-fed curiosity-seekers I guessed, stuck their heads in the door, wrinkled their noses at the smell, glanced around anyway, shook their heads at each other, then disappeared.

Then, abruptly, there was a clatter of motion. Guards everywhere, hustling us out of our cages, across the loading platform through a series of wooden livestock corridors—

One by one, we were all pushed through a decontamination tunnel. First we passed through stinging jets of hot mint-tasting water, then a cascade of billowing foam, then another hot stinging spray of mint-tasting water, then another kind of foam, then another spray—this one tasting of something like penicillin, only worse. One more wall of foam and a final spray—disinfectant-laced moisturizer. Probably some kind of antibacterial. They really weren't taking any chances here. And finally, blasts of hot air from the floor, the walls, the ceiling. If I'd had longer hair, it would have stood away from my head like I was a dandelion. I hunched and limped my way through that gauntlet as if I was in great pain and could barely move. Maybe they'd buy it. The only one who might know different had been dragged out by his arms. I didn't feel sorry for him.

At last, we all ended up on a brightly-lit platform, everyone naked, lined up like show dogs —or dead men waiting for the firing squad.

In front of us, a small gathering of men, all ages, all colors, all sizes and shapes. Various styles of clothing—as if each had come from a different civilization. Most of them looked well-fed. Fat. Spoiled. Puckered with sourful glee. Not surprising. Mom had told us once, "You want to put a man down in the gutter, you gotta go down with him to hold him there.

"There's a price you pay," she said. "If you're

shrinking another person's soul, you're shrinking your own at the same time. Once you get out there and start dealing with people, you'll see it. Again and again. There are people who have been hurt —and hurt badly—that's all they know, so they'll think life is about hurting people. They'll want to hurt you—and if you let them, then you'll want to hurt them back. You will. Just remember, everything you do to another person, you're doing it to yourself as well. You can't come home and say, 'Well, too bad. They had it coming.' Uh-uh. You don't do that. You come home and have a good cry about what they made you do, what they made you become to do it. You don't laugh, you don't celebrate, you let the hurt in, because otherwise you aren't going to be able to let it out again. You aren't going to be able to heal. And if you're walking around, hunched over in your own pain, you're no good to anyone. No good to me. No good to yourself."

Great words in the nice safe nest. Truly inspiring. But kind of hollow when you're standing naked in front of a group of pickle-faced men who are trying to figure out what you're good for. They talked among themselves, speculating, sometimes salaciously, occasionally pointing, and conferring with several dark-clad runners. Their laughter was ugly.

Few of them pointed at me—except to shake their heads disapprovingly. I had made myself pretty damn hideous. Right. Not even with a bag over my head. I hoped none of these guys were freaks for that. I was too small and wretched for any kind of hard labor. The best I could be —I assumed—was some kind of kitchen help. If you have to be a slave, the kitchen is one of the better places. You're unlikely to starve. As several excellent philosophers had pointed out, the goal of the slave is to eat as much as he can while doing as little work as possible—which is why slavery isn't a great economic model, unless you have a large supply of disposable slaves that you can work to death. I didn't think that was the case here.

A somewhat androgynous man of indeterminate age—ohell, he was an effeminate poseur in emerald vest and gilded tailcoat, a gaudy confection of jewelry and makeup, all topped with an elaborate hairdo—came strolling down the line, stepping carefully in shining high-heeled boots, peering at each of us through hand-held spectacles, shaking his head distastefully. He looked like the kind of French aristocrat whose head ended up in a basket in the Place de la Revolution while Madame DeFarge sat and watched, clucking with approval, and perhaps even losing count of her stitches in her excitement. I assumed this walking confection was the premiere buyer. Or maybe just the vendor. I wasn't sure.

He was also flabby. That was the ugly part.

He stopped in front of me, looked me up and down, then looked at me again through his glasses. Some kind of scanning device. He pursed his lips. He frowned. He fanned his face with a gloved hand. "Oh, my—" he said. In perfect Spanglish. "*Nada, nada. Esto nunca*. This will never do." He turned to an aide, there were several trailing in his wake. "*¿Es esto?* This is the one we were told about?"

The aide nodded. "Yes, m'lord."

The apparition turned back to me. "Either our little friend was hallucinating—or he beat this poor wretch into such an appalling condition. Fetch Dr. Grimes. I'd like to hear his opinion."

He moved on to the next, Talla-Talla. He studied him for a long moment, nodded, *tsk*ed approvingly, and went on. When he got to the end of the line, he spoke quietly with one of his aides. The man scribbled with his stylus on a black tablet, obviously taking notes.

When they finished, the aide gave directions to the guards and one by one, all the other slaves were marched off. I was left alone on the stage. Most of the crowd headed for the exits. Pretty soon, it was just me, two guards, two aides, and the walking wedding cake.

In short order, a very thin man in a black longshirt and tight black trousers arrived. And a string of pearls. Of course. What else with basic black? But he seemed very purposeful in his demeanor, so I assumed this was Dr. Grimes. He bowed respectfully to Monsieur Eunuch, as I had decided to call him in my mind, and then with a quick, "*Con su permiso*," he turned to examine me. "Oh my," he said. "Oh, my my my. I can see why you called me." He spread his hands wide and turned to the Monsieur. "I really don't believe I can do much with this creature."

Monsieur gave him a skeptical look. That was enough—

"What I mean, sir—" he hastily explained, "—is that it just wouldn't be cost effective. Termination is a much better option—" An even darker look from Monsieur stopped him mid-sentence. "But—but—if you insist, I will take a closer look." He fumbled in his bag for various scanning instruments, all of which looked much more sophisticated than Monsieur's Electric Spectacles. The one the Dr. ultimately selected looked like a flashlight with a hand-tablet attached.

"Well—let's see what we have here." He waved it at me, waved it again, frowned at the screen. "That's odd." He slapped the flashlight against his hand a couple of times, as if that would recalibrate it. He turned it off, listened to its sign-off beep, turned it back on, listened for its ready signal, waved it at me again, and studied the display with an even more puzzled frown.

Abruptly, he realized what he was looking at. His expression changed. He walked away from me and whispered privately to Monsieur Eunuch. Monsieur looked at me with a skeptical expression, then bent to listen even more carefully. They didn't know I could hear them as clearly as if I was standing between them.

"Monsieur, there are biological anomalies in this creature's metabolism that I would like to study further—at no expense to you, of course. I just need to make sure that he is not infectious, before we—"

"I paid in advance for a pretty boy, this *thing* is no pretty boy—"

"Yes, of course, Monsieur. You're certainly entitled to a refund of your deposit. I'll be happy to sign the provenance that this individual does not match the item described on the sales receipt. And uh, to be candid, you could still come out ahead. The onsite replacement will have a much greater value than this one and the one that was lost."

At last, between the two of them, they made a decision. Custody was transferred to Dr. Grimes — he motioned to one of the aides, who motioned to one of the guards, and they all escorted me out the door, through a series of corridors, and eventually to a set of chambers that looked like a medical facility.

It took a long time, because I hunched and

limped and staggered every step of the way. I even fell down a few times. By the time we reached the facility, I had a pretty good mental map of the path, steps counted, intersections, branching corridors, up-escalators and stairwells, and even a few suppositions about which way to go to reach the surface. I only look wretched.

Dr. Grimes escorted me to a med-chair, adjusted it to fit my twisted shape, and strapped me in tightly so I couldn't escape—at least, he *believed* I couldn't escape. I saw no reason to disavow him of that belief. Not yet, anyway.

He dismissed the guard and the aide, locked the door behind them, turned to a console and typed in some commands. I couldn't see the display. I assumed I was now being professionally scanned. This could be very bad news.

He pressed a key. Something buzzed. I went out.

TEN

I came to.

This room was smaller and darker. The walls were rough, unfinished. I wondered if we were inside a mountain, the whole space looked as if it had been carved into rock.

But I was still strapped tightly in a med-chair. And there was medical equipment everywhere. Mad scientist time?

"Ah, you're awake. How are you feeling? Never mind—I can see for myself. You're still a little blurry. That'll clear. You weren't out for long."

The voice was Dr. Grimes, he was somewhere behind me. "Say thank you. It wasn't easy getting you here."

That was not what I expected. But it was what I heard.

He was still talking. "Officially, you're dead. You died on the examining table. You were suffering from malnutrition, exposure, and hypothermia. Your heart couldn't take the stress.

Plus, I found some virulent bugs in your gut, just waiting to get out, so you had to be cremated immediately. I didn't even bother with an autopsy. Monsieur was very unhappy about that, but I put your ashes in a very nice jar and he put it on his shelf with the others. That satisfied him. He likes shiny things."

Abruptly, Dr. Grimes came around from behind the med-chair, stepping into the light so I could see him smiling like an old friend, "So, how's Mom? Is she still as lovely as a summer firestorm?"

I blinked.

"It's all right, Slither. I know who you are. And Mom's an old friend."

"I don't know what you're talking about."

"I'm talking about the lady who sent you to El Paso." He added, "Yes, we do have email here. And videos. You took out an assassin, you shifted to the Maria Hernandez identity, and they took you off the train somewhere in west Texas. Mom lost track then. She says she's sorry about that."

I studied the man. Either he was the real deal or Mom had a kaiju-sized hole in the organization.

"You don't believe me?"

"Why is a raven like a writing desk?"

"Because Poe wrote on both. Next?"

"Who sawed Courtney's boat?"

"It's 'Who *has seen* Courtney's boat?'"

"No, it was sawed in 1879. By Ned Hanlan's people."

"Or maybe even a Charles Courtney supporter."

"Charles Courtney wore a supporter?"

"I never seen it. Maybe it was sawed too?"

We both stopped.

"Do you trust me now?" he asked.

"Who are you? How did you get here?"

"I'm Dr. Edward Jackson Grimes, formerly of Tulsa. And yes I am a friend of yours. Also a friend of Bill W. and Dr. Bob. That's how I got here. I am a colleague, a consultant, and a communicator. Also an incorrigible punster, don't incorrige me, looking for the occasional partner-in-Grimes."

"You call that a pun—?"

"My sister makes an incredible clam chowder. It's so good, you pass out. She conchs to stupor. . . ."

"Manhattan or New England style?"

"You have to ask? Bad idea. Don't put all your begs in one askit."

"That's an old one."

"True dat. Indeed, so old it was fully groan."

"Okay, you can stop now. Before I change my mind about not killing you."

He held up his hands in mock surrender.

"I'll stop clowning around. Consider this a jester of friendship."

That's when I showed him how easily I could get out of the restraints. I stretched, straightened, swiveled my head to work out the last kinks in my neck—

"Point taken." He got serious again.

I let go of his throat. "How did you know I was here?"

"One minute." He reached around behind me, came back swinging a keyboard and display hanging from an overhead swivel-arm. He studied the screen thoughtfully. "Okay, according to the scan, you really are seriously malnourished and dehydrated. You've done a good job of not dying, but—hold on a minute." He stepped over to a closet, a large walk-in space, maybe more than a closet, and came back with a stack of high-energy bars and three large bottles of water. "You'd better start replenishing yourself."

He handed me the goodies—I started eating immediately. It was like chewing concrete. Around the third mouthful, I said, "You didn't answer the question."

"I was expecting you to figure it out yourself. Think about it."

I thought. I chewed and thought some more.

Apparently I wasn't chewing and thinking fast enough for Grimes. He said, "Listen. If Mom and I can send undetected messages back and forth through a chain of seven portals, do you think there's any security on *this* planet we can't tap?"

I held up the second ration bar—"You know, this stuff tastes like shit!"—and took a huge bite.

"That's 9,000 calories. Flavor was never a priority. And how do you know what shit tastes like—"

"Don't ask." I stopped to empty half a bottle of water down my throat. "Is the oxygen level in this room higher?"

"By twenty percent, yes. Mom needs you back in shape as quickly as possible."

"Why? Who do I have to kill?"

"That overstuffed turkey who bought you and would have sold you to the first buyer, if there were any, for starters. But there's a much longer list —"

"How soon? And why?"

"Interesting that you would ask those questions in that order?"

"I already have my own answer to the second one. How soon? And why do you want me to?"

"Yesterday. Because we want to stop a war."

"Here?"

"No. Back on Earth."

I stopped myself from taking the next bite. "Wait—" This was going to require some processing. *Ka-chunkita-chunkita*. Oh. "The war machines that Mac and his pa are testing—"

"Not just Mac. He's an outlier. There's about seven thousand of them. And they're not just testing. They're stockpiling and training. They've been planning for decades. Half a century. They're preparing an invasion."

"They're going to invade Texas?"

"No. Texas is going to invade the rest of the continent. This world—this whole operation, it's gearing up for an operation called Red Storm. They'll come in at the Waco Portal. Then—well, we're still not sure. They could go west, they could go northeast."

I thought about it. "No. They'll go east to gather volunteers from across the south, then they'll turn north, taking out the coastal cities to close off naval support. They'll sacrifice their local volunteers on the front lines."

"How do you know that?"

"That's what I'd do—"

"That's ugly."

"I'm not known for my looks."

"Not right now, no."

"You have local access. What does your intel suggest?"

"Straight north to St. Louis, then Chicago. Take out the hubs. Then east. They can advance quickly up through the center—"

I considered it. "No. That would leave them with hostiles on both flanks."

"Maybe. The other possibility is a western assault. Take out Pacifica. Despite the treaties, the eastern nations won't get involved. They'll hold an emergency session to deal with the crisis, demand a cease fire, try to negotiate a truce, and finally settle for economic sanctions. Oh, and they'll strengthen their borders. They'll make a lot of noise, but they won't counter-attack. They'll insist on negotiations."

"That won't work, will it?"

"Fanatics don't negotiate. And these particular fanatics have made it up in their minds that they're being oppressed."

"Are they? Being oppressed?"

"Most of them chose to be here. Except for the slaves, of course."

"Ah. So they're definitely oppressed."

"They think so. Paranoia is self-fulfilling." Grimes looked frustrated.

"You don't have enough intel, do you?"

"Nowhere near enough. We became aware of the situation much too late—way back when Grandma was still cooking. She smelled something burning and got suspicious—but by then they already had their primary channels buried and working. But she could still see that the wrong kind of machinery was shipping out. But with the regional breakup and reformation, she couldn't get in any deeper. Mom picked up the ball over a decade ago, but by then—" Grimes shrugged. "You can't see the elephant if it's been erased, but sometimes you can see the elephant-shaped hole it leaves behind. And sometimes you can even see the elephant poop on the floor. Sometimes you can follow the trail.

"We can track some of the embargoed gear in transit, but once it gets here, it disappears out somewhere, maybe to Oztralia, that's what we call the south island, but wherever it goes, it might as well be invisible. There are some tracking devices embedded in some of the machinery, but..." He shrugged. "No signals. Either they're finding them, jamming them, or simply shielding everything. But whatever they're doing, it's evidence they know how to protect themselves. Their tech is mostly brute force, but it looks like they're getting some advanced materiel from suppliers downline. They're trading water with one of the dune worlds who front for them. But whatever they're building out there—" He spread his hands wide in a shrug of helplessness. "This far out, they have complete freedom to build and test who knows what—maybe even nukes. We have some seismic evidence of testing. Whatever they're doing—it's all invisible. Which makes it hard to convince anyone there's a real threat. There's no evidence of buildup that we can prove. The evidence is mostly circumstantial, but it's compelling. If and when they do move, it'll be unexpected and it'll be a massacre."

"So we have to stop them here. Right? Is there a plan—?"

Grimes hesitated. "There will be—" He looked grim. "But first, you need to—" He looked me up and down, a little bit distastefully. "Well, do what you need to do."

"I need to rebuild."

"I see that. But not here—" His voice went grim. "We're heading into inner-summer and the scorch-belt will expand. This cave isn't deep enough and anyway—we can't wait out the summer. The invasion could launch any time. How fast can you bulk up?"

"Six weeks. Four if I fake it."

He nodded. "Too long." He puffed his cheeks, blew out his breath, a signal that he didn't like the decision, but it was the best choice possible. "There's a cot in the back. There's plenty of food and water. There's a shower."

"I have a plan," I said.

"You do? Already?"

"Yes. Take down the portal."

Grimes frowned. "It's not impossible. Technically the portals are fragile. In practice, they're so well guarded with so many fail-safes—"

"I know. And now they're stringing entanglements through them, so even if you take a portal down, the connection stays open, so it can be reestablished when the portal is rebuilt. So…I guess we'll have to nuke it."

"I think I have a couple of nukes in the back room, I'll have to check."

"You're kidding—"

"Yes, I am. What was your first clue?"

"You didn't use your serious voice. So you don't have nukes?"

"No."

"So where am I going to get some?"

Grimes shrugged. "I guess you'll have to borrow one of theirs."

"Yeah. That's Plan B."

"I don't see a way—" He shook his head in resignation.

"I'll burn that bridge when I get to it. First thing, I need mobility."

Grimes exhaled loudly, typed something on his keyboard, turned the screen around to face me. It was a biography, plus photos and med-scan.

"Can you become this person?"

"Probably." I heaved myself to my feet—I was still a little weak from the time-out buzzer, but I could feel the caffeine and the sugar and the stimulants in the energy bars starting to take effect. It filled me with false confidence. I peered at the display.

A man—of course. Middle-aged. Dark skinned, uncertain ancestry. Bland features, slightly uneven. Rough skin, patchy. Scruffy beard, otherwise bald. Slight strabismus. Broken nose sometime in the past. Weak chin. Vaguely unsavory appearance. Posture was weary, a little stooped. A paunch, not quite a pot belly. Flabby arms, fat legs. Slovenly. Herschel Trumb, Hirsh for short. The male version of Maria Hernandez, only worse. Easy enough.

"Is this a real person?"

"Not anymore."

"Disappeared?"

Grimes nodded.

"Do you have any voice recordings?"

"There's a complete bio-file there."

I paged through the file, skimming quickly. "I'll need to see how he walks, what his body language is. Who is he—I mean, who am I? What's my role here?"

"Drifter. Drunk. Circles around the edges of

things, never gets to the center. Not very smart. Looks at everything sideways. Doesn't listen, doesn't learn. Uses up oxygen. Nobody misses him. But he's useful for taking out the garbage—if it's not too heavy a load."

"And this is a good cover because—?"

"Because it's the only one we have."

"Really?"

"We have some fabricated identities. But I don't know if they'll hold up."

"I need something I can work with."

Grimes looked dubious.

"What?"

"Well, there is one—"

"Tell me."

"Finger. No last name. A disabled ranger. Walks with a cane. Won't discuss his past, specifically not the gimp. Some military and gang tats. Just came in from the Zona. Dissatisfied with the Union. Hoping to enlist as a trucker or a cargo-pilot. Some drug history."

"Real?"

"He was. He had dangerous skills with explosives. And he was one helluva sniper too. Bad news."

"Where is he now?"

"In the morgue. But his identity is

still banging around dogtown. He refused to rechannel."

"Lemme guess." I put on a southwest drawl. "If I ain't gonna let no salad-eatin', pickle-tit, turdle-faced socialeers tell me how to be, I ain't gonna let no wannabe Texas wienie-wagglers neither. Here I am, six foot two of pure mean cussedness. I c'n spit further than mosta y' c'n shoot. So, y'all just take me as I am, or don't take me at all. I c'n fight or drink, either's fine with me. But I ain't lettin' no one remap mah manhood. Me an' it have gotten along just fine for long enough, no need to change it up here. I still got a right hand an' a good memory." I looked to Grimes. "How was that?"

Grimes shook his head. "You're in the neighborhood, but that's way too polite for our man. And too sober."

"I guess I've spent too much time as a lady. I'll work on it."

"You'll have to. This one's a real piece of... something. Stupid enough to say what he thinks. Bragged about women—not a good idea here, and certainly not where he did it. He got himself beat up pretty bad—bad enough, they sent him to me. I get all the bad ones. Officially he's still recuperating. Critical internal injuries. He's up on the roof and we can't get him down. But I suppose he can still have a miraculous recovery. Let's say he got strong enough for surgery—"

"How long has he been lingering?"

"Five days now. I just haven't signed the death certificate."

"Uh-huh. So you were saving him for me, weren't you?"

Grimes shrugged. "I knew you were coming in. I was keeping my options open. But…this guy is trouble. Two days off the train, he's known as a bad'un. And now he's got a bullseye on his back just about anywhere he goes."

"But he can get inside, right?"

"A lot easier than Herschel Trumb."

"How convenient—"

"How soon? We need—"

Something clicked.

No, it was a lot more than a click—it came down with an ear-pounding *klunk!*

Grimes saw it in my face.

Sudden shock.

As the pieces fell into place.

"Ah, you figured it out?" Grimes laughed and looked at his watch. "Damn, girl! You did take a hit. You should have twigged it five minutes ago. Am I going to have to—*uhrk*, please . . . let go . . . of my throat—*ack* . . . if I can't . . . breathe, I can . . . explain —"

I let go of his throat. He dropped to the floor,

massaging his neck.

"You got any more of these things?" I held up the last bar. "I'm gonna need 'em."

"Yes, but—you don't want to overload your system too fast. You'll get a reaction—"

"I already had a reaction. You want to see it again?"

Still rubbing his throat, he said, "No thanks. I'll get you some more."

He came back with another tray of rations and more water. "Please slow down—?"

"I don't have time." I grabbed him and shoved him into the med-chair. I knew how this model worked. You can do a lot of painful things with it. "Now, talk. Why didn't Mom tell me this was the mission?"

He swallowed hard. "Because when you were captured, when you were scanned, if you had known—"

"I wouldn't have revealed anything—"

"She couldn't take that chance. Your involuntary reactions might have shown up on their scanners. They'd have killed you. We needed them to drop you here."

"That was even stupider than killing me—"

"They couldn't kill you on Earth. They couldn't take the risk. They were afraid you had implants they couldn't detect. But if you died here, whatever secondaries you might be carrying would go undetected."

"They underestimated me." No. "Oh, shit—"

"What?"

"We underestimated them! They could have killed me anywhere. They dropped me here for a reason."

"They want to know what you're capable of. Not you specifically—but shifters in general."

"Then they've been tracking me—"

"Yes, they were. The tracking device they implanted in you was destroyed when you were cremated."

"You got it out—?"

"I neutralized it in a way consistent with cremation. Unless they have some tech superior to ours, you're invisible again."

"What are the chances of that?"

"I'm not worried. These boys aren't very sophisticated. They believe in brute force. They prefer the sledgehammer to the scalpel and they don't care about collateral damage. We can see it in their planning."

"Okay, tell me the rest."

"Pods. Trucks. Measure how many have come through since the portal was opened— several hundred thousand. But the price of a truck or a pod-house is still too high. Scarcity.

Why? Our best intel—based on what they've been manufacturing, recycling, and rebuilding—shows they're repurposing a century's worth of trucks and life-pods into factories, supply depots, farms, processing centers—and armored train cars. We estimate ten thousand carriages by now. Maybe more. If even a thousand get through, they could cripple the North American Union. Mom doesn't want to take out the Waco Portal, it'll cut off a major branch, over a hundred worlds. But once those trains start coming through—well, that's the backup plan."

I was visualizing the problem. A long time ago—right after the Montana blowout—they stopped opening portals on Earth. Instead, you had to go to a secondary or tertiary world to open a new wormhole. The transfer world was usually a barren rock, at most useful for mining—but just as often an iceworld, there were a lot of those, and not all the ice was water, so those were convenient for gas mining, nitrogen, methane, ammonia, all useful. Even oxygen if you know how to crack the rocks. So raw materials were freely available for all kinds of manufacturing, and it didn't matter what kind of waste the factories churned out on dead worlds.

Viable planets were even more useful. They could host doorways to additional transfer worlds farther out. And eventually, those transfer worlds would open portals to even more inhabitable worlds—as many as practical, at least until the threshold of a stress-field blowout was approached—but that remained theoretically unlikely. Meanwhile, the starweb was spreading. One day perhaps, there might even be some understanding what worlds in this universe or whatever universes the portals we were actually accessing, what points in time and space—because no two worlds shared the same stars, none that were identifiable, implying that none of the portal worlds shared the same galaxy or the same point in time or even the same cosmos. Your guess is as good as the guesses of the most insightful astrophysicists. Meanwhile, the human species was expanding through the starweb as fast as portals could be opened. On a galactic scale, we were metastasizing. The supertrains ran through all the portals, the most cost-efficient way of moving large amounts of material across the worlds.

Worlds with pre-existing ecologies were often quarantined. The big fear was an unstoppable invasive species, any kind of virus, microbe, germ, or bug—anything coming back down the web. But not all the worlds were one-way. Colonies on barren worlds could have two-way traffic. Those venues were good for everything you didn't want polluting or endangering anything else. Vast farms as well—you didn't have to plow up forests and you didn't have to worry about predatory pests, all you needed was nitrogen and oxygen to start with and you could import those from iceworlds. So the commerce across the starweb was considerable. Ahh. That was it. The flaw in the plan.

I said to Grimes, "They'll be competing with a lot of other inbound traffic—"

"No, not if they take out all the other connections as they go, every line branching off the main trunk. That will give them a direct track all the way down to Waco terminal—unimpeded. Once they secure the line, they'll control all the traffic on the Waco branch—"

"So it's not just Earth—"

"Right. Waco is the primary portal, they have to secure it. But it's the whole arm they want. Every subsidiary portal. Every connection. More territory than a dozen Earths. But they need to own the Waco Portal, and that means taking out anyone who might object. The North American Union, for starters."

I sat down opposite him, staggered by the audacity of it. "That's one helluva power grab. You have to admire the insane genius." I did the calculations in my head. "If it succeeds, they get an instant empire. Instant control of all supplies, communication, access, everything. 'Follow our rules or we close your portal and you're completely cut off. Don't even think about counterattacking.'

With a single blitz attack, they'll have at least five hundred million people—maybe a billion, all of them effectively enslaved. Do I have that right?"

Grimes' expression was grim. "There's more."

"There's more?"

He nodded. "Worse."

"What could be—? Oh, crap. The women and children."

Grimes took a deep breath. He didn't want to say the next part. But he did. "Only half the children. And none of the women."

"Well, that doesn't make sense—"

"It does if you're insane. If your logic is warped." He gave me a sharp look. "Is it all right to get down from the med-chair now?" He didn't wait for me to nod, he eased himself to his feet. "I've been here more than a decade. That's more than long enough to understand the mind-set—it's even long enough to become infected with it. You start thinking of other people as the enemy, it becomes a self-fulfilling prophecy. I mean, you might be a man right now, but you're also the first woman I've seen since I emigrated fifteen years ago. If you weren't presenting as male, I'm not sure I would trust you. I'm not even sure I trust Mom anymore. They rechannel you here and—" He shrugged, embarrassed.

I didn't say anything. It was too much to

assimilate. I had to stop a war and my only ally had just admitted he couldn't be trusted.

"It's a monosexual culture," Grimes said. "They've been growing babies in bottles here for generations. They don't see any value in women."

"They're missing the best part of humanity," I said.

"Not in this mindset. If you're growing babies in bottles, all male, then women aren't necessary. They're an evolutionary handicap. Weak. Lousy warriors. Emotional. Too divisive for a stable culture. Pick your argument. Most of them are horse exhaust, but it's their ingrained reality. There's no one on the planet who's ever seen a woman. Women are monsters to them—there's a whole mythology of fear. And desire as well. And a lot of posturing and bravado. Some of those boys are already bragging about what they intend to do to any woman who gets in their way. It's ugly. You don't want to know."

"I saw Mac. More than enough."

"Not just Mac. All of us—them, I mean."

I didn't answer. Not then.

ELEVEN

Eleven days later, a certain deranged psychopath known only as Finger discharged himself from the infirmary and disappeared into the shadows of Dog Town, the most unsavory part of the settlement. And misnamed. There weren't any dogs here. Another thing wrong with this place.

A few hours after that, a skinny boy of uncertain parentage was seen scrabbling out into the desert where various nomadic tribes were rumored to harass unwary travelers.

An hour before dawn, an expensive male prostitute was seen leaving Dr. Grimes' private quarters. He caught a rental cab and headed toward the Celebration District.

An hour after dawn, an unidentified slave worker exited from the service wing of the compound, wearing a backpack. He disappeared into the early crowds of slaves gathering in the marketplace, where the day's commerce would be turned into the evening's meals.

And so the day went, with various identities

coming and going—only a few more than usual.

And except for Finger, who would be useful as a distraction, none of them were real—all the rest existed solely as simulacra in the digital realm. Whatever agencies might track these identities would be chasing ghost trails that would lead ever farther out into the wilderness before evaporating. Their attention would be everywhere else. Their attention would occasionally flicker over several other identities—which were real, but were so much like the ephemeral ghosts, they too would eventually be dismissed as irrelevant.

Meanwhile, Dr. Grimes himself left on errands of his own in the early afternoon. Well, it looked like Grimes. A casual observer would have assumed it was him. Even someone who knew him well would have been fooled for a few moments. Possibly longer, depending on the relationship.

It had taken me eleven days to de-uglify myself. I used that time to scour his files and learn what I needed. Nowhere near as much time as I would have liked, but enough.

The late Dr. Grimes had made a critical error —he didn't know how quickly I could bulk up if I had to. And I had to catch him by surprise.

No, I hadn't told him the truth. That's one of the things about shifting—a shifter never lets anyone know what she's really capable of. Grimes' machines had been easy to fool, I'm designed that way. They hadn't shown how I had compressed most of my muscle mass—and certain metamaterials can't be scanned easily, but underneath the stringy skin and some layers of greasy fat to simulate atrophied muscles, I had a core of densely compressed me. Expanding myself to fill out the phenotype of Dr. Grimes was mostly a matter of taking in enough water to flesh it out and enough fuel to activate it.

Terminating Grimes was a double necessity. First, he couldn't be trusted. And second, he couldn't be trusted. That I didn't like him very much only made the task all the more enjoyable.

Okay, yes—there was a slight chance I was wrong. But there was a much larger possibility that I was right.

Grimes had to be the reason why so many of Mom's previous attempts to insert an agent here had failed. He found them, earned their trust, then betrayed them—whenever it was convenient, whenever it was necessary, whenever he needed something from whatever this particular conspiracy called itself, Operation Red Storm and its wannabe Caesars—and especially whenever one of those agents got too close to the truth about Dr. Grimes, someone died.

This time, it was Dr. Grimes. No tears for traitors.

I couldn't leave his body where anyone

might discover it. Grimes' co-conspirators would realize immediately that Grimes had been killed by an agent—and therefore, there was an agent on the loose. Me.

So I ate his liver—and all the other musculature I needed for additional mass and fuel. The rest went through the crematorium—along with the real Finger. Some people get queasy at what a shifter is capable of. Those people aren't shifters. I had a job to do, I couldn't afford to be nice about the details.

The immediate problem was that all of the identities in Grimes' portfolios were set-ups, Finger in particular. Grimes had been pointing me toward it from the beginning. So I had to ditch it as fast as I could—and in a way that would suggest I'd been killed in the process.

None of the identities in his database were acceptable. I had to assume they were all tainted. So either I'd have to twin someone—or go off the grid entirely. Both options were dangerous.

If I wanted to twin, I had exactly the person in mind. And I had a pretty good idea how to get in. Grimes had kept exquisite files. Part of being a double agent is knowing when and how to blackmail someone. Grimes had used his medical expertise to implant his own tracking and surveillance chips in everyone who sat in his med-chair. (I'd already neutralized the chip he'd placed in me. And several others that he had missed when he'd scanned me—chips that had been added at various steps along the way, by Mac, by the slavers, by the traders, by all the people who had earned themselves a special place on my list. I expected to be very busy in the near future.)

Grimes had accumulated enough information to reveal levels of corruption almost all the way to the top—almost, not quite. If you're at the top, you don't need Grimes. But instead of disrupting the power structure, he'd used his information slyly—instead of a hammer, he'd used a scalpel, keeping himself safely insulated against whichever way the political tides were flowing.

I toyed with the idea of publishing those files. There was too much to send to Mom—and I wasn't sure I could trust Grimes' claim of a private network. He might not be the only double agent on this side of the portal.

On the other hand, publishing those files across the starweb would certainly trigger an emergency quarantine. The portal would be narrowed, key sections of track would be disabled, the invasion wouldn't be stalled. But I'd have to get to the portal itself to get that information out.

It was an option, but not the best. The political reactions were unpredictable. Therefore dangerous.

Chaos is never the best option. You can't know what the unintended consequences will be—worst possible case, it accelerates the catastrophe.

Just the same, I was already pissed off enough to consider it a worthwhile option. I have both slaves and slaveholders in my family tree, so I'm not unbiased.

TWELVE

Monsieur Eunuch's real name was Barron Bn Bloatherd. Something like that. I might have misspelled it. I was beyond caring. He died quickly. I would have preferred that he died painfully. I would have preferred that his death could have lasted several days. I've heard that it's possible to prolong a death for longer than that, but that's not termination, that's torture, and I don't believe in torture. It's a bad relationship. It's that thing that Mom said—about having to go down there in the gutter with the other guy.

Anyway, Bloatherd died in bed. He almost died in his sleep, gurgling horribly the whole time—but he came awake in one final instant of awareness, his eyes suddenly wide in terror, as he tried desperately for that one last impossible breath. His face turned red, then redder, then purple, then at last a kind of blue-gray pallor began to appear. His heart stilled, his blood settled, and his mouth sagged open, his gray tongue protruding slightly.

I held the silk scarf tight around his neck

for another hundred count—he was dead, I was certain of that, but I don't like slavers, and I was savoring the moment.

The other complication—the prettyboy curled up next to him, barely pubescent, remained peacefully asleep. I'd shpritzed them both with sleepytime as soon as I'd entered the room. In a few hours, maybe a little longer, whenever someone got curious enough to wonder why the surveillance cameras were glitched, there would come a knocking on the door.

With no one answering, they'd have to force their way in, where they'd find three household guards sprawled in the foyer in the early stages of decomp, all with their throats neatly slit from left to right. Further exploration would reveal the Barron's bloated body sprawled across the silk sheets of his enormous bed. If they were recoverable, the household surveillance videos would reveal that one of the two Barrons had strangled the other—

Impersonating the Barron hadn't been hard. He wore makeup, jewelry, occasionally a rebreather, and usually peered at the world through augmented glasses. His ornate wigs had other augments, he was a walking data mine. The Barron was taller than me, I'd need to work on that, I didn't have a lot of time to stretch my bones, fortunately he had an entire wardrobe of high heels, so that helped. Fortunately, he wasn't much bulkier. I filled out my face and arms, I could use padding for the rest.

I could pass for him at a distance, I wasn't sure about a close examination, but I wasn't planning to let anyone get very close. An excess of his worst perfume would certainly help. I did check to make sure it was a socially appropriate fragrance. This world had some interesting cultural artifacts.

Prettyboy was another problem. His bracelet said he was the property of a whoremonger of some repute, as much repute as any whoremonger could be said to have. So that was my first visit. I dropped off the boy at his owner, then—using the Barron's own credit—I bought his freedom in grateful appreciation for the excellence of his service. The boy continued to sleep through the whole business, something the whoremonger did not question. Apparently the Barron wasn't the first who preferred an unconscious partner. I watched while the whoremonger removed the slave bracelet and replaced it with a freedom chip, thanked him and told him I was leaving on a long journey, but I would see him when my business was concluded, he could count on that.

I was tempted to use the Barron's credit to free all of the whoremonger's boys, but that would have aroused suspicion. It would have also set the whoremonger on a search for new slaves. I thought about killing the whoremonger instead, but that would just pass his slaves onto someone else, possibly someone worse. Mom always said, "You can't fix the whole world. Fix the parts you can and move on. It's gonna hurt, but you're no use to anyone dead."

I had maybe twelve hours, maybe more, maybe less—until somebody somewhere knocked on the Barron's door, looked at all the surveillance, put one and one together, and realized there was a shifter on the loose. At that point, things would get spectacularly crapalicious. I'd have to work fast.

I only needed to take care of two pieces of business—one very necessary, the other because justice required it.

The first, I purchased Mac. Well, the Barron purchased Mac. That was tricky. Mac should have been scheduled for cleanup and auction and rechanneling. Instead, he was languishing in cleanup. There was an administrative hold on him.

Getting that hold released required a substantial bribe, and a lascivious wink— a deliberate hint that the Barron had some specifically lustful intentions.

Fortunately—well, not fortunately, more a matter of convenience, I had the Barron's own records as my resource—the little bureaucrat behind the desk regularly performed these kinds of favors for the Barron. He was happy to do a little business on the side. There was no shortage of customers for prime specimens, customers who preferred not to be seen at the auctions. He was happy for the business, the percentage received was always higher than what they would have earned from an auction.

I sold Mac to the whoremonger. Not for very much. Mac wasn't exactly a bargain. Reprogramming that nasty piece of manmeat was going to be an expensive effort. Never mind, the whoremonger was happy to pick up Mac at his convenience. I didn't ask what he intended to do with him. I doubted there would be any shortage of customers, probably even a few former colleagues. Mac had metaphorically screwed a few who might be willing to return the favor physically.

I wasn't worried about Mac's feelings in the matter, he hadn't worried about mine. Perhaps I should have. I still had a small kernel of moral integrity somewhere in my soul. I just hadn't used it in a while. I did have some body issues, it's hard to be a shifter and not have issues, in my case it was physical assaults and violations. I had long ago stopped worrying about that—unless it was my own body being violated.

Being an operator meant living outside.

Outside everything.

Because assassination is not about what the assassin might think about assassination. No.

It's simply about getting the job done. Quickly. Efficiently. Invisibly. And that meant giving up any other kind of thinking.

It's not just part of the job. It's the whole job.

I would have liked to have put some of my specialized skills to work. This world needed someone like me. Someone to take out the trash. I wanted to do it too.

I could have climbed the ladder of authority, job by job, man by man, all the way to the top. But it would have taken too long. The scale of the task put any possible completion somewhere on the other side of impossible. There were just too many. And based on the evidence, the commitment to war was so thoroughly embedded into this culture that it wouldn't matter how many I stopped. There were too many eager replacements waiting for their own opportunity to be The Man. As much as I would have enjoyed it, it wasn't going to work. And even if I could create a real fear in what passed for leadership here, there wasn't enough time.

Nope.

Plan A.

A simple slice of the scalpel. This monster had to choke to death on its own blood.

But even the simplest slice of any scalpel requires that the scalpel holder knows how to wield it.

I had to do some serious data diving and dark-web spelunking. Grimes had developed enough deep access to make it practical. I found what I needed. I did what I had to do. Chaos was possible. I made it inevitable. Just not yet.

And no, I'm not a nice person. I've occasionally pretended to be, but I'm not.

Assuming that I'm tractable is the mistake the late Dr. Grimes had made. And Mac. And a long list of others. Operators aren't just smugglers. We're assassins by necessity. And occasionally cannibals. And a few other things even more distasteful. We are specialists in disruption and revenge. We do the things we do because they have to be done.

Because those dear sweet idealists who believe in ethics and morals and integrity will always be prey for those who don't.

I—and others like me—we are the necessary monsters, we're the guard dogs who patrol the fences so those dear sweet idealists can continue to believe in ethics and morals and integrity. And maybe someday...yeah, I'm not holding my breath either. We're all human. That's the problem.

That said...there was still one thing I needed to do. If only to prove I could still pretend I could be something more than just another killing machine.

The Barron already owned Talla-Talla. The

tall, strange man was scheduled for a requisition center, a polite name for a refactory, where he would be reconstructed as a mindless killing machine, then shipped off to some secret training center on the other continent. It's fascinating what you can discover with unrestricted access to a culture's dirtiest secrets.

Pulling Talla-Talla out of the requisition center would raise some eyebrows, might even raise some questions, but I was willing to take the risk. It wasn't going to be the biggest risk I was taking.

I arranged to have Talla-Talla delivered to a slave transport service, then had the service transport him to a cage in the belly of Barron Bn Bloatherd's private carriage. Then I arranged to have the carriage attached to an outbound train, one heading to the dune world where the Barron conducted occasional business affairs, apparently with the emphasis on affair. Most of this I could do online. Hiding my tracks should have been the harder part, this was a world populated by paranoids, but I did have some skill in the matter.

Talla-Talla had been drugged. He was now an ambulatory corpse, a zombie, barely conscious. He followed without words. Whatever was feeding the drug into his system had been implanted deep enough that I might need specialized equipment to find it and remove it. But in the meantime, he followed and that was enough.

The important thing was getting us both to the other side of the portal—before the Barron's body was discovered.

Once we pulled out, once I no longer needed his identity, I started pissing and shitting as fast as I could. I probably overloaded the recycler unit in the carriage, but I needed to shed the unnecessary bulk and reinhabit one of the false identities I'd inserted into the system.

Then there was the problem of Talla-Talla Manfella. I finally decided to put him in cold sleep. The Barron usually kept a couple of prettyboys in storage when he traveled, but the caskets were empty now. And if they hadn't been, I'd have paid for two more freedoms.

We weren't going far, only three stops down. Two of the stops were barren transfer worlds. One was cold, the other was hot. In both cases, the atmosphere was unbreathable. We had to stay in the carriage. Not a problem, the Barron had a well-stocked larder. I skipped the alcohol and drug cabinets, raided the closets for appropriate clothes and decorations, and shifted my features to match.

The third stop was Barlow, the dune world that fronted for Sparta—and several other inhabitable branches. Barlow had a very profitable business, ordering, transshipping, trading, and manipulating the economies of seven other worlds. They had their own nasty little corporate empire—a relationship that existed only as long as Sparta found it useful, and the more I prowled through their records, it was apparent that they were well aware of the dragon at their doorstep.

Something else I found, the Barron had his well-manicured fingers deeply embedded into a lot of ugly little piles here. That was useful too. I might have to get my hands very dirty before I could get clean of this place.

Barlow was desolate. Dirty red sand out to the horizon, an uneven rocky plain in all directions. A dim sun low in the distance. A scattering of moons moved slowly across the sky, each in their own low orbit.

But the air was marginally breathable. Vast forests at the poles were finally producing enough oxygen that the atmosphere was the equivalent of eight kilometers above sea level on Earth. A little thin, but not impossible. I could wear a rebreather. Not totally necessary, and a bit uncomfortable, but it covered the lower half of my face.

Eventually, the train slid into the long, covered trench that served as a station. Most of it had to be dug several layers deep into the ground to avoid the high winds and dust storms. Not surprising, the Barron's carriage was met by a squad of hulking warriors, all armed and armored, so identical in appearance they could have been clones. Maybe they were.

The airlock door popped open and I picked

my way gingerly down the stairs as if this kind of reception was not only normal, but to be expected. I knew how to be fabulous and was almost grateful for the opportunity. "Oh, thank you for greeting me. Thank you. This is my first trip here and I'm not sure where I have to—oh dear me, is something wrong, sir?" The man who stepped forward was almost as wide as he was tall. Except for the silver insignia, he wore a uniform so black he looked like a blot in the air. And his weapon was pointed meaningfully at my chest. Not my most vulnerable part, but a part I am still somewhat fond of.

"Barron no more. Much dead. Who you?"

The faceplate of his helmet was blank, except for my own reflection, so I played my part to the mirror. "The Barron is dead? Oh, no, no, no! That can't be true. I just saw him yesterday and he was very much alive. Very much, I can tell you that. We shared a bedboy, a pretty little redhead, very pneumatic. And the Barron? I can tell you, he was as vigorous as a teener. Impressive. Really. No, he's not dead, not at all. This is a horrible joke. I'm sure you must be mistaken." I pulled out a silk handkerchief to mop my face. More performance while I scoped my surroundings and whatever avenues of violence might be necessary. But my performance was working. I fluttered and flustered like a hyperactive butterfly.

The gun barrel wavered.

"Please, put that thing away. I work for the Barron. Perhaps you've seen my signature on some of the transfer papers. I'm the Second Associate Deputy in Charge of Whatever." I offered a well-perfumed hand. "And you are?'

The man stepped back, away from my deliciously elegant gesture. He didn't raise his faceplate and if he had a name, he wasn't going to share it. "Identify self," was all he said.

"I thought I just did. Oh dear. Oh. I see. Yes. My validations. I have all that right here, wait a minute—" I fumbled at length inside my robe. I had layered myself well from the Barron's extensive wardrobe-fabber. I clashed in multiple layers of high-heeled boots, leggings, pantaloons, longshirts, cummerbunds, waistcoats, vests, dickies, pendants, wigs, bonnets, and wraps. And jewelry. Earrings, bracelets, rings, pendants, ankle chains, ornate belts, everything. I had no intention of skimping. What would a junior deputy wear if he intended to impress anyone with his presumed importance? Also a great way to transfer wealth.

But the real intention was to demonstrate that this flubbering popinjay was annoyingly incompetent, no threat to even the most suspicious observer. A minor lackey.

Oh, yes—but with a thick layer of personal armor under all the performance. Just in case.

I finally decided which deputy's identity

to produce and pulled out the appropriate set of data cards, authorizations, confirmations, and validations. Deliberately trembling, as if I had finally realized the danger I was in, I passed them over. If I had done my job right, they would pass even a rigorous inspection.

I had done my job right.

The big man studied the cards, scanned them with suspicion, some kind of military device —I waited patiently, putting on a performance of boredom bred from familiarity with the workings of petty bureaucracy until he finally grunted something that might have suggested he was satisfied. He barked something in a language I didn't recognize and all of his clones lowered their weapons.

I mopped my face furiously. More performance, but also a bit of additional defense against the omnipresent cameras. "It's so dreadfully hot out here, is there someplace cooler we could go? And please tell me why you think the Barron is dead. I just can't believe it."

He hesitated, communicating with a superior perhaps?

Right. He was just following someone else's orders.

Abruptly, the squad surrounded me, ushered me off the platform, into an elevator, and down several levels to a holding cell. I could have gone into triple-time and taken them all down, but there was no need. Not yet. But I was getting back to full capacity, so it was an interesting thought problem, not a specific goal.

I sat alone, locked in the holding tank for half an hour. As cells go, it wasn't a bad one. There were several chairs and a desk, so it was obviously used for interrogations. The lock on the door wasn't unbreakable, but I was still playing stupid. Someone, somewhere, was trying to figure out who I was and what to do with me. Sooner or later, they'd try to interrogate, so I ran my own scenarios, practicing my spontaneous responses.

Finally, the door opened and three serious-looking men marched in. They arranged themselves on the far side of the desk and frowned at me. The one who was obviously in charge, glowered at me. "All right. Who are you? Really."

"I thought you'd never ask," I said. I stood up and began peeling off the layers. I started with the jewelry, earrings, bracelets, pendants, tiara, combs, belts, chains, and so forth, placing each item deliberately on the desk in front of them. For those who might value such things, it represented a small fortune in shiny metal and colorful stones. I noticed their reactions. Yes, they were interested.

The robes followed, the pantaloons unzipped, the waistcoat, the chemise, all of it—until I had finally stripped down to the basic black armor underneath. "Ah, this too." I passed across another set of identity documents. "Lieutenant Colonel Wright of the Dark Order, Second Squad."

"The Dark Order?" The man blinked.

"We've never heard of it," said the man to his left.

"Of course not. If you had, it wouldn't be dark." I pulled up my chair and sat down again. Now we were equals, facing each other across the desk. "You already know that the Barron is dead. What else do you need to know? I must inform you up front. There are some things I cannot discuss."

The shift in their posture told me what I needed to know. The man in front of me had authority. He said, "I'm Colonel Spender. I run security for this station. We sent a message upline that the Barron's carriage had arrived. We received an immediate reply. The Barron was dead and we were requested to secure any passengers and wait for further instructions."

"Do you follow every order that comes down from Sparta?"

"We cooperate as much as we can."

"Is that alliance official? Or just a convenience?"

He ignored the question. "What do you know about the Barron's death?"

"It was well deserved," I said.

"We heard he was killed by a shifter."

"Yes," I admitted. "That's the cover story."

"Eh?"

I looked up at the ceiling, as if I was conferring with a superior officer, as if I was deciding what to say next. I looked at his associates, then back to him. "Can we talk?"

"Would you feel more comfortable if they left?"

"It might be appropriate. I promise, you will not need your bodyguards."

"Are you that dangerous?"

I pointed toward the corners of the room. "You have multiple weapons pointed at me and you have a button hidden in your ring. You still don't trust me. But I have given my word. You can trust that."

He nodded to his associates. "I'll be fine."

We waited until the door closed behind them.

"All right," he said. "Who are you? Really."

"Doesn't matter," I said. "I'm here. You're there. We both need information The real challenge will be whether or not we can trust the information we're about to trade."

"You said the shifter is a cover story."

Ah, thank you. I know which way to go now.

"Yes. The truth is much worse." I spread my hands as if about to reveal something serious. "There's a faction. Not quite a resistance movement, but it has the potential to become one. Sparta is mostly empty. There are too many places to hide things. We've depended on that ourselves. But this movement is something new. We have a few prisoners to interrogate. We will find out how deep it goes, but it will take some time. But at the moment, you can understand why it's necessary to establish increased security up and down this branch of the line. At some point, you will be further informed about what is required—"

"You're imposing martial law?"

"Not yet, but if necessary, yes. And this is strictly need to know, not to be shared outside of this room." I nodded toward the hidden cameras. "I assume you can erase those recordings?"

He grunted and I continued. "We have some concerns that knowledge of certain operations may have leaked downline. It is possible that a necessary element of surprise may be lost. We need time to investigate. We may need to adjust our plans, possibly a postponement, possibly an acceleration. I'm not part of that decision-making process. I just do my job." I met his skeptical gaze. "Meanwhile, the shifter story is a useful justification for our investigations. The rumors are a convenient distraction. You do understand."

Colonel Spender considered my words.

"The rumors are very convincing—"

"They should be. My division planted them."

"And you expect me to believe you? What if you're the shifter?"

I shook my head in amusement. "Do you really believe those silly stories about super-augmented body-changers? If I really had that kind of ability, do you think we'd be sitting here talking?"

"You don't believe in shifters?"

"I think it's all psy-ops. Stories they spread to keep us looking over our shoulders and distrusting each other."

The colonel leaned back in his chair. Was he relaxing finally? "It is an interesting possibility," he admitted. "But the Barron is still dead."

"Yes, he is. I killed him myself. And faked the surveillance video to support the shifter story."

"He was useful," said the colonel.

"He was dangerous. He was channeling information to the resistance movement. He was doing it through the boys he slept with. He loaded critical information into their slave bracelets. We don't know how much the boys might have known. We think not much. The slave owner retrieved the data from their bracelets and somehow sent it downline. We don't know what channel he used, but we do know what data was leaking. We have agents downline. We know that operators were being sent upline, but we have high confidence that all of them were identified and neutralized before they could even confirm their arrival on Sparta.

"Meanwhile, we are now in the process of deciding whether to shut down the procurer or use him as a channel for false information. We have to determine what he sent and what they know. So the Barron would have been a problem. He would have passed that information to the resistant faction. It gets complicated. His termination was a matter of some discussion." It was a delicious fabrication, but convincing enough to buy me time —and if Colonel Spender believed it, his life as well.

"You now know as much as you need to know." I hoped it would be enough. If he were to pass a recording of this conversation back to Sparta, a certain whoremonger would be out of business. A small step, perhaps. Maybe. I'd never know.

"So you killed the Barron."

"Somebody had to do it."

Colonel Spender took a deep breath, as if he was about to close the deal. "You have a body in cold sleep. Is that the shifter?"

I shook my head. "No. He's something else. A mutant? We don't know where he came from or what he is. Some kind of adaptation. He's not a shifter, but he is something unknown. He probably was dumped into one of the pods of contraband we allow. I was taking him downline to a more advanced facility for examination. The Barron's carriage was a convenient cover."

"So you want me to just let you go?"

"Is there a reason to detain me?"

"I should send you back. That would be safest."

"And if you're wrong? What if my superiors are unhappy with that decision? How safe would that be for you?"

Colonel Spender didn't answer. "You are quite the problem, aren't you?"

"Not necessarily."

He nodded. He glanced at the pile of jewelry on the desk.

"Keep it," I said. "It's the Barron's and he doesn't need it anymore. Neither do I."

"Go on."

"Put me back onboard the Barron's carriage and send it downline."

"How does that help me?"

"By the time you got all the separate incoming messages sorted and read, the carriage was already on its way."

"That would require some serious data

hacking of the timestamps."

I gave him the skeptical look.

"It's not impossible," he admitted.

And we had a deal. The rest was details. He was a weasel and weasels are useful.

Not fanatics though.

The difference between a fanatic and a weasel is that a fanatic is so completely embedded into a cause that they can't think about anything else, while a weasel is always watching out for their own best interests. That's why weasels are better. They can be used.

THIRTEEN

While the colonel was arranging things, so was I. The dune-world's data security was not secure enough to justify the word security. Well, not for me. I had the right augments and I was able to dive deep enough that I had a fairly clear picture of the seven branches up from here.

It wasn't good news. They were all part of the same conspiracy to invade. A couple were allies of convenience. Geographically they didn't have a choice. But the rest were allies of intention. And that clarified my options.

This whole branch had to be cut.

There are ways to cut a branch. Some are permanent.

But there are always consequences. The intended consequences are chosen, the unintended show up right behind them. And in this case, the question was impossible to answer easily.

If this branch was severed completely,

isolating the seven populated worlds up the line, would they survive? Could they achieve self-sufficiency among themselves. I ran the numbers and survival of the outer branches wasn't impossible, but it would require a level of partnership that none of these worlds had yet demonstrated. Partnership requires more than need, more than advantage. It also requires mutual respect.

The question is always the casualty rate.

And in this particular case, it was the size of one disaster measured against the much larger size of the potential disaster that might happen if I didn't act.

Mom wasn't here. I couldn't ask her. Nobody was here except me.

If it was merely a question of personal loyalty, the answer was obvious.

But this wasn't just a question of personal loyalty.

I had been trained to leave my ego at the door. My emotions were merely my ego in disguise.

Cut the infection. Save the body. That's what any surgeon would say—based on the assumption that the body is worth saving. Well, hell, I had to believe that, didn't I?

But the casualty list upline—?

The only one there I felt any pity for was

the sleeping prettyboy in the Barron's bed. But only because I wanted to assume he was an innocent. Maybe he would have hated me for breaking his rice bowl and turning him free without any other skills he could sell? Maybe the prettyboys have all been rechanneled to embrace their situations? I hadn't considered that, but it probably made sense. Maybe my own few remaining scraps of morality had forced that decision.

I didn't know.

I'd seen only the smallest part of Sparta. I had no idea how common its thinking was. But even that smallest part, it could have been forgivable, I'd seen worse. But I also had to consider the much larger parts I'd discovered in Grimes' lab, and in the Barron's suite—

Just browsing through his closets, his medicine chest, his collection of sex toys, and finally the menus for his fabbers, was an education in depravity. I'm not against diversity. Normal diversity. I even respect kink. Most of it. But there are limits. Really.

Or maybe that's the last desperate bit of my latent morality. I just don't believe in hurting other people—unnecessarily.

But I'd also seen enough to know what Sparta's rulers intended.

This was necessary.

The thing is, people can be good. Most are.

Governments only pretend to be good. Even the good ones.

At least, the bad ones are obvious. There's that.

I can process a lot of data in a very short time. I can visualize graphs and trendlines and even the effects of certain kinds of black swan events. I can see the possibilities and the consequences.

And I still make stupid mistakes. Because a large part of me is still human. The important part. Because if I lose that, I lose me.

It didn't matter how many times I looked at it from how many different perspectives—I had to consider it it as fairly as I could, but each time I came up with the same ugly answer.

The carriage slid across a medium-sized world baked by blistering sunlight. Through a portal and into permanent darkness, a rock floating so far away from its primary that its sun was only a speck of brightness gleaming among the rest. So of course, this place was simply called Rock. Its gravity was miniscule, I didn't walk, I bounced.

As expected, the carriage stopped, conveniently shunted to a siding while more important portal traffic passed. On the other side of this downline portal was another lifeless rock, equally airless and uninhabitable. It was called

Hard Place and it hosted upline portals to a dozen other branches, far enough down that they were not allied with Sparta. So it had to be a primary target for the invaders. They needed to capture it to restrict the traffic from the other branches. Because they would be sending at least ten thousand carriages, they needed total control of the line, no interruptions. They would have to repeat the process, seizing three more branching worlds downline and they already had teams in place ready to act as soon as the first invasion trains started arriving.

But this portal, between Rock and Hard Place, was the critical one. The invasion had to start here. Every train from Sparta and its allies had to funnel down through this portal, across to the portal that led into Hard Place and from there down to the inner part of the starweb. And Earth.

I couldn't act while the trains were moving through. I'd have to act during one of the maintenance breaks. Every twenty-first hour the system was paused for thirty minutes while the bots ran tests for physical confidence of the tubular rails. The station had enough equipment and supplies for even the most severe of breaks. Usually everything was five by five, but repairs would extend the break as long as necessary.

I could do something about that, of course. I could break something.

Rock didn't have a big station, didn't need

it. Rock was an intermediate, it had only one upline and one downline, and one small structure for local operators. A cluster of portal pods had been converted into a monitoring station and residences for the maintenance team.

The portals were always housed in huge containments, horizontal cylinders designed to withstand even the most severe blowouts—even on an airless rock like this. Opening a new portal was always a gamble. The Montana blowout proved that. No matter how carefully the equations had been designed, there was also the Murphy factor. A new portal could open into a gas giant, with its high-pressure atmosphere roaring out in an unstoppable torrent. Or worse, the portal could open into airless space and your own atmosphere would be sucked away. Even a small atmospheric difference was enough to justify a series of airlocks. Every containment had a built-in self-destruct that would automatically trigger if the portal opened disastrously—which is why airless transfer stations like Rock and Hard Place were valuable. Once established, the airlocks could be left open. Trains could slide right through. Simply faster.

Unfortunately, the self-destruct charges were no longer necessary here and had been removed for reuse elsewhere.

Not a problem. There were six other ways to disable a portal.

Which is why they were usually well-guarded.

The airlock of the Barron's carriage had mated to an airlock and service tube where the carriage could be recharged and refreshed and take on supplies if necessary. A maintenance tunnel connected all the access stations. At least a dozen trains could be held on sidings until there was a necessary break in traffic. Most travelers stayed in their carriages, the station had few amenities to justify the long walk.

I wasn't interested in the amenities.

The lighter gee made the job both harder and easier. Everything bounced. Interesting, but I'd already adjusted for that. I went into triple time and caught them by surprise. Four were on shift. Three were sleeping. The last five were in the galley. I broke two spines and crushed three windpipes. I crushed the skulls of the two I threw against bulkheads. One made the mistake of reaching for his gun, I made him eat it. He put a splatter of brains and blood on the wall behind him. Finally, I sliced the throats of the three sleepers. That was eleven. I found the last one hiding in a closet. I shoved him out an airlock. I hate cowardice.

A quick exploration revealed the bodies of the downline crew they had killed. They had been tossed into a freezer compartment. If I had seen them first, I wouldn't have been as considerate to the Spartans.

Back to the control room, the trains were still running. The station was designed to run itself on automatic. It was unlikely that anyone would come either up or down to investigate until several critical messages went unanswered. I had time, just not enough to waste.

I went back to the Barron's carriage to restore myself. Triple time creates a massive energy debt. I needed energy. Food. Water. Electrolytes. Vitamins. Batteries. Ideally, I should nap, but not yet. I could run on fumes if I had to. I'd just need more time on the other side. But if I had time to recharge, I was going to take it.

I checked on Talla-Talla. He was still alive. That was something. The monitoring data was skewed, so I had no idea if the casket was wrong or if there was something odd about Talla-Talla's biology. I assumed it was him. Whatever he was, that was a question I didn't know and I couldn't assume. I just knew I owed him.

Maybe on Earth. Maybe Mom had the resources to figure him out.

Getting down to Earth—not impossible. Despite the severe proscriptions on importing organic material of any kind from the outer branches, there were still ways to get back. If a traveler had spent the entire journey inside a sealed capsule and worked only through external bots, they were still considered clean enough to return.

One last task. I still had time.

Demons.

A demon is a software entity that can hide like a trojan, spread like a virus, and prowl through a system like a worm. It stores itself as multiple individual pieces that only occasionally reunite to go to work, so it's incredibly hard to find, even harder to remove, because each piece is hidden and disguised and has the ability to recreate all the other pieces.

Demons are nasty pieces of work. These were set to go off only on Sparta and only after the portal was destroyed. They would seek out the most secret data, wherever it was stored and republish it to every public channel, making it impossible for anyone to keep anything hidden. The best way to stop a conspiracy is to shine a light on it.

I hoped.

Human beings can be damned contrary.

I'm still human enough to know that much.

But maybe that's the essence of humanity.

Hope.

The last curse out of Pandora's box.

I mean, think about it. Who would put hope into a box of curses if hope wasn't also a curse?

It's another word for wishful thinking.

I hope I get results.

These are the things I think about while I'm waiting.

It wasn't a long wait.

The portal schedules updated. A longer than usual train was coming downline from Sparta.

Only one?

Of course.

They only needed to report the one. After their teams took control of Rock and Hard Place, the following trains would have a clear path. They wouldn't need to schedule them.

Perhaps the Barron's death had accelerated their plan. Or maybe it was the lack of response from the team on Rock. Whatever, they couldn't wait any longer. The invasion was coming.

Right. I was out of time.

I monitored my breathing. I was as ready as I was ever going to be.

Time to finish the job.

I ordered the carriage to start downline as soon as there was a break in traffic. And there was going to be one very soon. The Barron's carriage had a complete data dump. Whatever happened, whether I succeeded or failed, downline needed to know. Perhaps they'd get the message in time.

I popped out of the airlock and headed into the maintenance tunnels, but this time the equipment bay. Through the airlock and into one of the tractors that served as bulldozer, forklift, and service bot. It had three sets of waldos. It wasn't designed as a weapon, but if you knew any of the vulnerabilities of the target, the tractor could do some serious damage.

I drove it hard, bouncing across the uneven surface of the rock toward the upline portal, occasionally firing downward-pointing rockets to keep from bouncing off. Gravity here was almost insignificant.

I found a place at the base of the upline portal, just beneath the tracks. All I had to do was push the anchoring frame off base.

The last few carriages from the other branches came sliding through. Invasion supplies or routine cargo? Hard to tell. I had to let it go. Maybe it would be evidence.

The tractor's display updated the portal schedule. The clock was ticking. There's a question. Do clocks still tick? I'd think about it later.

I had time, maybe enough. Portals have to be spaced apart, something about stress field disturbances, so the Spartan train had a lot of kilometers to cross before it reached the portal to Rock.

Inside the open space of the containment, the portal was a circle of light. I could see clearly through it to the other side, the interior of the protective containment on dune-world. Trains would have to separate into smaller linkages to pass through a series of three airlocks, then reform here.

The portal itself had no material structure. It was simply a hole in space. But it required an anchoring ring around it to hold the tracks in place. The anchoring ring was held in place by six tubular stanchions, two at the eight o'clock position, two more at six o'clock, and the last two at four o'clock.

These were my targets.

I rolled the tractor forward, set its anchors, and used the heavy-duty waldos to grab one of the four o'clock anchoring stanchions. Pushed it hard —it resisted. It wouldn't pull either. Nothing. The base of the damn thing was buried too deep and the tractor didn't have the leverage to dislodge it.

This job required something more immediate.

The stanchions were thick tubes of polycarbonized steel, embedded with crystallized nanowires, one of the strongest possible combinations of fabricated materials, a state of matter somewhere beyond hardened ceramics— not impossible, you just had to fracture the bonds on their helical axis, you could break the matrix.

So I armed the cutting torch.

In the vacuum of airless space, the flame of the torch was almost invisible. But I could see a line of darkness forming on the white enamel of the stanchion. It spread slowly, widening and stretching—a little more, almost halfway around, and then abruptly, the stanchion snapped.

The second stanchion was only a meter away. I grabbed it with the waldos and swung the torch around. Again the dark line spread slowly across the bright circumference of the tube. Again, it snapped with a soundless crack. The edges were clean.

It wasn't enough. The four remaining stanchions were still holding the ring and its tracks in place, two at six o'clock, and the two at eight o'clock. I still had time.

The two supports at six o'clock were thicker. They took longer. Too much longer. The ring was now held in place only by the supports at eight o'clock and the tracks that came through, but it was still enough to keep the ring centered around the portal—and time was getting tight.

Drove around the base to the last two tubes. They were as solid as the rest. But the cutting took longer. The torch was running out of power. Only got halfway through the last one before it shut down completely. And the airlocks at the far end of the containment were cycling.

Grabbed the last stanchion with the heavy-duty waldos, set the anchors and applied full power to the download facing rockets. And pulled.

The stanchion did something it wasn't supposed to do, something it wasn't designed to do.

It bent. I leaned on the controls and shouted, screamed every curse I knew in seven different languages. It must have worked. The ring tilted sideways off its base, almost thirty degrees. It pulled the tubular tracks into a rollercoaster twist. Not enough yet. The trains would twist, but they could pass.

Pulled again. Invented some new curses.

The stanchion couldn't bend any further. If there had been air on this rock, I probably could have heard it groaning. I angled the rockets for additional thrust—and abruptly the stanchion broke and the tractor was jerked backward, held in place only by the last two anchors. They screamed in protest. I heard the sound as a physical sensation transmitted directly through the cables. The tractor vibrated with it.

Rolled back to the ring and pulled it further to the left. It rolled slowly and the tracks resisted as they turned forty-five degrees off horizontal. They must have groaned, I couldn't hear them, I just kept pulling.

Upline, at the north end of the containment, the multiple shields of the airlock were sliding open, revealing the first cars of the invasion train. They rolled forward and I turned the tractor's rockets up and sideways and pulled again at the ring. It jerked and twisted and the tracks finally pulled apart.

The engineer must have seen the derailment ahead. Sparks poured from the leading carriage's wheels as he desperately tried to stop, but the momentum of the rest of the train behind kept pushing the lead car forward.

Another desperate yank at the ring, another hard jerk—it lurched sideways hard—and abruptly, finally it was no longer centered around the portal. Only half of that hole in space was visible in the ring—and the tracks were now completely cut off, disappearing somewhere behind the portal's right edge.

And still, the train came plunging forward, the cars pushing forward—with no tracks to guide them, they bumped and banged into the ring, shattering pieces off of it—or into the shimmering edges of the portal where the abrupt discontinuity scraped away the bellies of the first carriages and the sides of the ones that tumbled after. The parts that came through fell slowly to the surface of Rock, crumpling and bouncing in an unhurried gavotte of destruction.

There was no stopping it. The momentum

of the forward cars pulled the following cars into the growing debris field of wreckage. The edges of the off-center portal sliced them open, decks and bulkheads and material peeling off into the upline side, while other huge sections kept sliding forward. And as the tracks tilted more and more sideways, out of sync with the portal, the discontinuity was carving even huger gaps out of the side of each car that attempted to pass. The lights of the train flickered to reveal startled men flailing in sudden surprise as their bodies exploded into the dark vacuum.

And it all happened soundlessly.

Finally, at last, no longer held in stasis by its protective ring, the portal began to shrink.

It wavered and wobbled and with every progressive uncertainty, its diameter decreased. The hole in space was closing—

Unable to stop, the rolling train kept coming, each carriage sliced into smaller and smaller cylinders of debris, until—

The portal winked out.

Where the far end of the upline containment had been, only the uneven landscape of Rock and the distant emptiness beyond.

At last, everything was still and silent.

The debris field stretched halfway around Rock, with pieces still falling slowly to the surface. Perhaps some of them would fly away into space.

Others might fall into close or distant orbits. I didn't really care. I wasn't planning to stay.

I drove the tractor toward the downline portal as fast as it would go, occasionally using the rockets to lift it above the carved path that was supposed to serve as a road.

Something familiar up ahead. I recognized the red and gold trim. The Barron's carriage had not gone downline. I climbed back up through the belly hatch and peeled myself out of the suit.

Oh.

Without a proper manifest it had been directed to a siding. There, see, I'm not perfect. I missed something. I filed it and we rolled. Through the downline portal to Hard Place and from there...the inner connections of the starweb. It would take a while. There was a lot of traffic stalled here, piling up. Unable to go north, it would have to return somewhere south. Some of it would be useful. Some of it would be evidence.

I was tired. I needed to rest. Emotionally too. I made coffee. I sat. I closed my eyes and cried. A long time.

I had to mourn.

Not just the deaths I had caused, not just the destruction—but who I had to become to cause it.

I had to get it out of my system—that gleeful enjoyment of revenge, that self-destructive belief that those poor fools had deserved what I had done to them.

I didn't know them. I didn't know who or what they were or might have been. Given better circumstances, they might have been better people. Given better circumstances, I might have been a better person too.

But they weren't and I wasn't and this was what happened here.

It hurt.

I had to heal, whatever it took to get back to who I wanted and needed to be. It was going to take a while.

Fortunately, I had time. A lot of it now.

But I had done my job and I should be able to get home from here. Eventually.

And I'd shift back to female again. After my experience with the men of Sparta, I wasn't sure I ever wanted to be a man again. But maybe that was part of my healing too.

Someday, though—when I was ready, I'd march into Mom's office and report to her in person. I figured she had some serious 'splaining to do.

Oh, one more thing.

I put my coffee down and went to check on Talla-Talla.

His recovery chamber was empty. He was gone.

According to the records, the casket hadn't been opened since I'd laid him in it.

It didn't make sense.

Later, maybe.

Only a feeling.

But lying on the Barron's luxurious bunk, I'm not fussy—the feeling became a conviction.

Talla-Talla wasn't us.

I had no evidence for this. It just felt right.

But maybe he was another kind of operator —an observer from somewhere else, as far advanced beyond me as I was advanced beyond unaugmented human beings.

Maybe he was there to see if mere humans were learning to be more than mere.

I couldn't know, but it was a nice thought.

It was something to hope for.

I hope I passed the test.

Maybe hope isn't always a curse.

I hope I live long enough to find out.

THE BOY WHO WAS GIRL

ABOUT THE AUTHOR

David Gerrold's work is known around the world. His novels and stories have been translated into more than a dozen languages. His TV scripts are estimated to have been seen by more than a billion viewers.

Gerrold's prolific output includes stage shows, teleplays, film scripts, educational films, computer software, comic books, more than 50 novels and anthologies, and hundreds of articles, columns, and short stories.

He has worked on a dozen different TV series, including *Star Trek, Land of the Lost, Twilight Zone, Star Trek: The Next Generation, Babylon 5,* and *Sliders.* He is the author of *Star Trek*'s most popular episode "The Trouble With Tribbles."

Many of his novels are classics of the science fiction genre, including *The Man Who Folded Himself,* the ultimate time travel story, and *When HARLIE Was One,* considered one of the most thoughtful tales of artificial intelligence ever written. His stunning novels on ecological invasion, *A Matter For Men, A Day For Damnation, A Rage For Revenge,* and *A Season For Slaughter,* have all been best sellers with a devoted fan following. His young adult series, *The Dingilliad,* traces the healing journey of a troubled family from Earth to a far-flung colony on another world. His *Star Wolf* series of novels about the psychological nature of interstellar war are in development as a television series.

A ten-time Hugo and Nebula award nominee, David Gerrold is also a recipient of the Skylark Award for Excellence in Imaginative Fiction, the Bram Stoker Award for Superior Achievement in Horror, and the Forrest J. Ackerman lifetime achievement award.

In 1995, Gerrold shared the adventure of how he adopted his son in *The Martian Child,* a semi-autobiographical tale of a science fiction writer who adopts a little boy, only to discover he might be a Martian. *The Martian Child* won the science fiction triple crown: the Hugo, the Nebula, and the Locus. It was the basis for the 2007 film *Martian Child* starring John Cusack and Amanda Peet.

Gerrold's greatest writing strengths are generally acknowledged to be his readable prose, his easy wit, his facility with action, the accuracy of his science, and the passions of his characters. An accomplished lecturer and world traveler, he has made appearances all over the United States, England, Europe, Canada, Australia, and New Zealand. His easy-going manner and disarming humor have made him a perennial favorite with audiences.

David Gerrold is the 2022 winner of the Robert

A. Heinlein Award.

BOOKS BY THIS AUTHOR

Praxis

A lifetime in the Labor Corps—or colonize a new world. For Jamie and José, not much of a choice. But Praxis wouldn't be easy. To survive there, you had to depend on each other. And that requires honesty that few possess. Praxis is a bold experiment in society building, a monosexual colony, with no promises of survival and no return trip. But it's got potential. You just have to build a new civilization—on the other side of the universe.

"A wonderfully realized and self-contained story about sexual ambivalence (amongst many other things) that nevertheless leaves you hoping Gerrold's next SF tale picks up where this one leaves off."

—Nigel Suckling, Hugo-winning author

"*Praxis* is one of the very few books I've read where the premise of the society/world/universe is so interesting that it engages regardless of the plot. And the plot is a novel and unusual possible human situation, driven by the constraints of what may well come to pass, where traditional space opera is dragged screaming and kicking into a future with brand-new conventions. What *Praxis* is really (as is all the best SF), is the intro for a never-ending epic. But the evocative set-up is what I look for in speculative literature—and this book serves as a magnificent springboard for the reader's imagination."

—F. J. Bergmann, SFPA Grand Master & editor

"The thought-provoking story of two partners set to embark on a one-way trip to a planet that's all men—a literary exploration of human relationships in a brutal society seeking to colonize the universe."

—Dr. Daniel Pomarède, co-discoverer of the Laniakea Supercluster, the South Pole Wall & the Dipole Repeller

"Master of the imagination David Gerrold does it again, *Praxis* is a story of letting go, communication, and acceptance. For men to find a new way they must first redefine manhood, break from an oppressive society, and together learn what it means to become a new type of human."

—Jean-Paul L. Garnier, editor of *Star*Line* & *Simultaneous Times*

The Man Without a Planet

The Man Without a Planet is a science fiction reimagining of the classic tale, *The Man Without*

a Country—Redmonde had found his niche in the glitterships of high society, reveling in the opulence and gamesmanship it afforded, until a sudden regime change leads to his permanent exile in the far reaches of space aboard starships building a network of portals through the cosmos. He will never be allowed to see his home world again and escape would seem to be an impossibility—but when the opportunity presents itself, Redmonde disappears into legend.

"In *The Man Without a Planet*, David Gerrold has given us an ambitious reinterpretation of a classic. In this engaging science fiction retelling of *The Man Without a Country*, we find the main character, Redmonde, negotiating the sharp edges of his quarantined banishment in deep space and the intersection of his personal belief system with the sledgehammer of an imposed political ideology."

—Katerina Bruno, science fiction poet and 2022 SFPA Dwarf Stars Award finalist

Here There Be Lawyers

Dar is a well-connected arbiter and Turtledome is comfortable enough. But the colony on Praxis requires his expertise in crafting a constitution —and he doesn't really have a choice in the matter. Their objective is a bold one, and if they succeed, powerful interests and a highly lucrative, intergalactic economic system will be disrupted. Permanently. A world is at play, the stakes are high, and a corporate overlord will stop at nothing to protect its investment.

FORTHCOMING BOOKS BY THIS AUTHOR

Praxis II: Praxis Makes Permanent

The Praxis Papers (Praxis I & II)

The Girl Who Was Silver

Available everywhere that really good books are sold.

Thank you for purchasing this book.